Just Des(s)erts

By

Fiona J. Roberts

A Tree District Books Publication

Tree District Books, LLC is the publisher. It holds the license with respect to this work and any derivatives. Please email cmbenza@treedistrictbooks.com for more information.

ISBN-13: 978-1-7327168-6-5

Chapter 1

Looking down on the corpse, knife in hand dripping blood, Eve felt good. An article in a magazine that provoked an, interesting, discussion, had led to this. Who knew that a chat over Sunday lunch between Eve and her friends Dorothea and Penny would have led them to this point. It was remarkable and most satisfying.

Eve left her two-bedroom 1950s bungalow at a quarter to twelve for her friend Dorothea's house. She would arrive at about the same time as Penny who was coming from the opposite direction. The ladies had lunch together every Sunday and rotated the cooking duties between them. It was always a pleasure for someone else to be doing the cooking, but Eve particularly liked eating at Dorothea's because she would invariably serve up a spicy Caribbean dish. Dorothea's home also reflected those Trinidadian roots, decorated in bright colours enveloping you with warmth the moment you crossed the threshold.

They were an unlikely trio who had been brought together by tragedy. Their husbands had been businessmen who had invested in, what turned out to be, a Ponzi scheme. Most of their savings had disappeared, along with the fraudster, leaving them in financial hardship. Long comfortable retirements to villas in sunny climates were just shattered dreams. As businesses folded and assets were liquidated, the lives of all concerned were changed forever.

The three ladies followed a well-honed routine. A cup of coffee and the Sunday papers were the first order of the day. Interesting articles were mentioned and discussed before lunch was served around one o'clock. Eve, at fifty-two years old was youngest of the three and had an enviably slim figure. Her hair was cut at the local salon into a short crop which she dyed blonde herself using one of those kits. Gone were the days when she would languish at the hairdressers for half a day having it all done for her.

Dorothea was a statuesque woman of sixty who, at five foot ten, towered over her two friends. She had been the positive force that had kept them going when things had looked so bleak after their losses, although it had been hard for her too. Penny was fifty-five and, she would say, slightly overweight. She was absolutely convinced that her friendship with these two ladies had saved her life.

"I swear to God that you look thinner every time I see you while I get fatter." Penny was looking Eve up and down. "How do you do it?"

Eve gave a wry smile. "Ah, the secret diet. It's called nervous energy and not being able to afford a car so you have to walk everywhere."

"Don't worry Penny, I'll give her extra today and try fattening her up," Dorothea chipped in.

They thought they were being financially responsible by investing for their futures. They were persuaded to invest in a fund managed by someone who had worked as a trader in the city. Some of the money would go into bonds and some into stocks and shares. They were told it was a balanced portfolio and relatively low risk. The money was never invested. They received dividends taken from the money invested by others, reassuring them that everything was fine. It was not.

Those first few weeks after the discovery of the con brought pain, anger and sorrow, but these were just the tip of the iceberg. As Eve's husband Frank closed the warehouse that housed his small wholesale clothing business for the last time, he seemed to throw in the towel on life too.

Three months later, he died of a massive heart attack. Dorothea's husband, Royston, was a manager at an insurance company. He started as a clerk after leaving school and had reached the heights of senior management, much to the pride of his family. A couple of months after the loss of their life savings, he was diagnosed with prostate cancer and succumbed quickly. Would he have fought harder for his life if he hadn't been conned? Dorothea thought that he would have. Poor Penny, hers was the most desperate story of them all. Her husband Derek had taken their losses very badly and more or less stood back and watched as their catering business faltered due to his inability to take any action. When it finally folded, he folded too. He was found slumped over his steering wheel in the garage. He had died of carbon monoxide poisoning.

The perpetrator of the crime, Martin Cole, had been caught on the Costa del Sol and returned to England for his trial. The three ladies first met during preparations for the court case. They gave testimony about the promises that were made, the money that was lost and the devastation to their lives. Martin Cole had many other victims but these three widows would provide the heart wrenching stories that resonated with the jury and skewered the accused. He was sentenced to five years in prison. Any hope of recouping some of the money by seizing his assets was quickly dashed. He was gambling addict and most of the cash was gone.

Eve sold her large executive home, paid off the creditors, and bought the small bungalow. She was now working at the department store where she used to shop. Entering the job market after so long away with limited computer skills had meant that she could not be choosy. At least she got a discount on the clothes when she could afford them. Penny had downsized as well to an apartment supported by a small pension from a previous job and hand outs from her children. She also worked part time for an accountant, the same accountant who had looked after her husband's business and introduced them to Martin Cole. He employed her to shuffle papers out of a terrible sense of guilt. She was not in a position to reject his charity.

Dorothea was the most fortunate financially. She received a death in service benefit from her husband's company and also a widow's pension. She had her own pension from her years working as a teacher as well. But she too decided to downsize her home as her children were no longer there and, like her friends, had relocated to a part of town where the properties were smaller and more crammed together. They now lived close to each other, handy for their Sunday lunches.

Chapter 2

Martin Cole visited Eve and Frank at their home following a phone call about his high yield fund. He was aware of the adage that if something looked too good to be true, it probably was, so he had promised better than average returns rather than excessive ones. He wanted to appeal to executives and small businessmen who were somewhat financially aware.

He was a tall and rather gaunt looking man. His hair was cut short in a classic man's style with a side part making him look older than he actually was. He took a great pride in his appearance wearing a tailor made suit, bought when he first started working in the city as a trader, and a crisply ironed shirt and tie. The older people he targeted were more likely to trust a man wearing a tie. His shoes were buffed every morning before he left home.

He was so wrapped up in his scheme that Martin sometimes forgot to eat. He relied on the tea, biscuits, and cake that he was offered throughout the day by his clients. He liked to be slim but he was beginning to look cadaverous. Tonight, he must make an effort to eat something. A starving financial adviser didn't instil much confidence.

As he told the couple about how their money would be invested and the dividends they were likely to receive, he would produce a glossy brochure featuring graphs and a whole lot of jargon. He talked briefly about his successful career in the city as a trader but mostly he let them talk. People liked to talk about themselves and he paid close attention to what they were saying.

Most of what his clients told him was boring, but he would remember snippets of conversation about family or businesses which he would quote back to them at the appropriate time. This habit reinforced the customer's impression that he was a thoroughly decent and caring man. He talked to Frank about golf, which had been mentioned several times in their conversation and said that he was keen to learn. He was so busy managing his fund that he barely had the time for any leisure pursuits. He was caring and conscientious.

The headed paper, bearing a crest and the requisite details of his membership of various financial bodies, confirmed receipt of Eve and Frank's money and assured them that Mr. Cole would be taking personal care of the funds. The letter was a standard format that he used for all customers but he personalised each one with a brief hand written note. On their letter, he wrote "Hopefully one day I'll get onto a golf course."

When Martin met Penny and Derek he knew that he had his work cut out. Even though he had been introduced to them by their accountant, Derek was still cautious. As he listened to Martin's sales pitch, Derek took notes and asked a lot of questions. This sale had certainly kept him on his toes. Had the inquisition gone on for much longer he might have given up and walked away. In the end, Derek had taken the plunge and closed the deal over a cup of tea and some homemade cookies.

The receipt for their money arrived from Martin Cole and Penny and Derek remarked at how sweet it was that he had handwritten a note at the bottom. It said "Usually I just send a cheque for the dividends but I may hand deliver yours if it means I can have more cookies!" What a nice man he was.

Dorothea and Royston knew that their retirement would be comfortable. She had worked as a teacher for many years and would receive a pension and he was due a good pension too. They had savings to take a bit of a gamble with so they agreed to see Martin Cole. He arrived for his appointment a few minutes late saying that he had been waiting to hear the test match score on the radio, so sorry for the delay.

He knew that the couple had Caribbean roots and he had taken an educated guess that cricket would be a good topic of conversation. He had been right. He listened to the story of how they had met at a match in which Royston had been playing and that he was a great catch. He laughed at the pun whilst grimacing inside. The stories of how couples met were near the top of his list of things he hated. He also hated pets that came near him, photographs of grandchildren and holidays, and questions about himself.

The number of people who offered up a daughter or friend upon learning he was single was legion. He had never really wanted to be in a relationship or get married. He had taken girls out for the sake of appearances but he wasn't that bothered. He wasn't interested in men either. He thought of himself as asexual. He had neither the time nor the inclination to pursue romance. It was like his indifference to the food. He had no desire for pleasures of the flesh he just desired possessions.

The letter which arrived at Dorothea and Royston's home following their investment in the scheme had featured a small drawing of a ball hitting a wicket next to Martin's signature. It made them smile and they commented at how considerate he was to take the time to add this personal touch.

As soon as the money came in, it was allocated for specific purposes. Some was put aside to cover the dividend payments. Some was spent on items that Martin needed, like a car. The rest of the money was drip fed into the hands of Martin's bookies. The empire had inevitably collapsed, and Martin had fled He landed a job selling timeshares in Marbella and had made a few sales when the authorities had caught up with him.

The Spanish police found him in a hall which was staging a timeshare event and dragged him out in front of his colleagues and potential clients. In Spain, the police had guns so he didn't even attempt to put up a fight. He was held in custody whilst his extradition was arranged and then put on trial.

Martin Cole pleaded not guilty and prayed for a miracle. When Dorothea, Eve, and Penny had finished giving evidence, which included the details of their husbands' deaths, he knew that the miracle wasn't going to happen. He was sentenced to five years. He would have to be locked up with common criminals and eat terrible food. Poor, poor Martin. What a nice man he was!

Chapter 3

The smell of the Caribbean spiced roast chicken filled the kitchen as Eve, Penny, and Dorothea sat at the table flicking through the papers. It was two years after the trial had ended but they were all still troubled by what had happened. One of the magazines that came with the papers featured a photograph of a model making an undignified exit from a taxi.

"It may be undignified," said Eve, "but she still looks great."

"And thin," added Penny.

Dorothea peered over their shoulders, "Look you can see her pants. At least she's got some on I suppose."

Further on in the magazine was one of those true life stories which featured a woman who had been conned out of money by a man she had met through a dating site. They all paused and reflected.

"There's always another crook trying to con someone out of money." Dorothea shook her head as she read.

"Another bastard you mean." Eve's lip was curling.

"Brings it all back doesn't it." Penny took a deep breath to control her emotions.

The story told of recently divorced, forty-seven-year-old Patricia. Her husband was having an affair with a younger woman. Her confidence had taken a hammering but she was beginning to put her life back together. Her friends encouraged her to join a dating agency and she had eventually and reluctantly agreed. She put a photograph that was taken in flattering light on the profile and lied about her age. She wasn't expecting Prince

Charming; she wasn't expecting anything at all but to her amazement, she got some replies.

The magazine detailed the way the conman had drawn her in with lies.

Patricia went on a couple of dates with men who had obviously lied about their ages too and then she went on a date with Simon Butler. He let her talk about her life and he sympathised when she told him about her ex-husband.

"How could he leave someone like you?" he had said. "He should have realised how lucky he was to be married to you." He gazed into her eyes and held her hand and kissed her cheek when he walked her back to her car. He insisted on paying for dinner. What a nice man he was.

They had been on four dates and then he phoned to say that he would not be able to see her for a few weeks.

"Oh no, why?"

"Patricia, it is nothing you have done. I, well, I'm not really able to talk about it. It's rather embarrassing."

"Simon, don't be silly. You can talk to me about anything. Tell me what the problem is."

"Okay. The thing is, I am a bit short of money at the moment. It's a temporary situation. My uncle died and I will get a large sum of money from his estate. I've spent out on some stuff I needed, and on taking you out, and now there has been a delay with the legal side of things. Another few weeks and it will all be sorted."

"Why does that stop us seeing each other?"

"I can't take you out and expect you to pay. That is not what a gentleman does."

"That's very noble, Simon. I know you are a proud man, but I am happy to pay. You have been so generous to me and now I will be generous to you."

As she looked back now, Patricia could see how foolish she had been. She had said of course she would pay for their dates. When he asked to borrow a small amount of money, she thought nothing of it. As the requests for money came thick and fast, she just kept handing it over. When he asked for another £5,000, she had said it would be difficult. He had pouted and whined that she didn't love him because if she did, she would find the money. Finally, Patricia had come to her senses and she told him that actually, no, she didn't love him. He left slamming the door behind him and was never seen again. He had got away with £23,000 which she had no chance of ever getting back.

Simon Butler was arrested, taken to court and convicted of fraud. He was given a sentence of two years. The article said that he had been released after serving a year of his sentence. Patricia said that serving a year in prison was not enough of a punishment for what he had done to her. She suspected that there were other women he conned in the past and that he would be looking for new victims in the future.

As he sat in prison, Simon was just biding his time until he could get out and resume his career of stealing money from vulnerable women. A prison sentence was an occupational hazard for him. He would not be rehabilitated; his criminal career was simply paused until he was released and could start again.

Chapter 4

"It makes me so angry every time I read one of these stories," Penny voiced what they were all thinking.

"I know and when they are caught, they just get a short prison sentence," Eve shook her head at the reality of the justice system.

Dorothea paused in her preparations, "Like Martin Cole."

They all sneered at the mention of his name.

"I could quite happily murder that man." No one disagreed with Eve.

Dorothea served up her lunch of chicken with sweet potatoes and sweetcorn and the conversation on subject of Martin Cole continued.

“The trouble is,” Penny said, “if Martin Cole was murdered, we would be quite high on the list of suspects.”

Dorothea joined in the speculation, “I read somewhere that the majority of killings are carried out by people that are related to or know the victim.”

Eve looked disappointed. “I’ll have to take it out on someone else then. What about that Simon bloke from the article in the magazine? Maybe I could kill him.”

“You would be doing all of womankind a great service but the trick is not getting caught.” With this comment, Dorothea began the debate of whether they could “get away with it” or not.

They began with a list of potential risks and Penny got up, grabbed a pen and paper, and began to take notes. There were the obvious risks. You didn’t want to be caught in the act. Someone could witness the murder or place you in the vicinity of it. They were already using the vernacular. There was of course DNA, fingerprints, and even shoe prints. If you researched anything to do with the murder on the internet, a trail would be left. If you bought anything from the internet that was used in the murder, that would also leave a clue. And then there was CCTV and mobile phones which could indicate that you were in a particular area. A bottle of wine opened and the discourse resumed. Having identified all the pitfalls, the next thing was to get around them.

"I think the fact that one didn't know the victim is the biggest advantage. Then, if there are no physical clues, no one would suspect a complete stranger." Eve looked at her friends who nodded in agreement.

Penny suggested that the time and place of the murder were crucial considerations. A murder shouldn't be carried out in front of a lot of witnesses in broad daylight, for example.

"The best thing is to catch them with their guard down, possibly at home," Dorothea mused.

"When they've just got out of the bath, naked, and exposed," Eve said with a delighted grin.

"We could leave some sort of mark or use a signature style that would declare that women had been avenged," Penny giggled. "Like Zorro."

Dorothea frowned at them and reminded them that anything like that would constitute a clue.

At which time the discussion became an actual plan to murder to murder a man on behalf of all women none of them could remember. Their telephones buzzed all through the week as they thought of more problems and solutions and, when they met the following week, each of them clutched a notepad containing their thoughts and ideas. The usual trawl through the newspapers was abandoned as they had more important things to discuss. The mood around the table was serious as they assembled their notes and then looked at each other ready to begin.

Dorothea opened the discussion. "As you know, I hold Martin Cole responsible for the death of my Royston. If we can stop anybody else from falling victim to one of those low life con artists I am all for it. I personally, however, don't think that I could deliver the coup de grace. I am more than happy to aid and abet in the planning, providing an alibi and anything else that is required."

"I've thought about this all week. Something needs to be done about these people. In my mind, I can imagine finishing some cheating scumbag off but I may feel differently when faced with the reality," Penny said.

Eve had no such qualms. "I am quite happy to be chief dispatcher. All I need to do is conjure a vision of Martin Cole's ratty face and that is enough. I'll get it done."

The decision had been made and the roles had been cast. They were doing this for themselves and every other man, woman, or child who could be affected by fraudsters, fraudsters who went to jail for a couple of years and then came out and did the same thing all over again. It would be a selfless public service. They had finished with speculation and theorising and now they needed to move forward. It was Eve's turn to cook lunch and after her traditional roast beef and Yorkshire pudding, they would start making a proper plan.

Chapter 5

All through their lives, Eve and Frank had been hard workers. They got up early and attacked every day with purpose. Between them they had built up a small business importing and selling sportswear. They supplied some independent shops and a small chain as well as outlets at sporting venues such as golf clubs and gyms. Frank was a keen golf player and Eve had tried playing but it had not been for her. She didn't mind him playing because it kept him fit and active. She could put up with the golf anecdotes if he bought her lunch every Saturday in the smart clubhouse at the course where he was a member.

Competition from the internet and the recession had made things difficult in the last couple of years but they had been sensible and saved for both their retirement and any financial downturns. They had decided to clear their accounts with some of their suppliers and scale back the business slightly. If they specialised, they would not have to keep so much stock. It was when they contacted Martin Cole to make arrangements to withdraw some of their savings from the scheme that alarm bells began to ring.

Frank called Martin and, when there was no reply, he left a message. The next day, he phoned again. After five days, Eve had driven to his office to talk to his secretary thinking that maybe he was on holiday. When she found an empty room with a pile of unopened post littering the floor, the panic started to set in. As she turned to walk away, a member of staff from another company in the building stopped her and advised that she was not the first person to come looking for Martin Cole. She drove back to their warehouse desperately trying not to panic but, on seeing Frank, she lost it completely.

"He's gone." Eve repeated the words over and over again.

"Who has?" Frank asked.

"Martin Cole. I think our money has gone too."

They sank into chairs in the office and stared at each other in disbelief. Eve described the state of his, former, office and the encounter with the person who had given her the bad news. No one in the building had seen him for at least three weeks.

Frank finally broke out of his inertia and picked up the phone. "I'm calling the police."

And so, the nightmare started. They called their accountant and advised him of what had happened and asked him for options to help them get out of their sudden, and very worrying, financial woe. The police interviewed them, for the first time, later that day and, as they told their story, they felt so foolish for placing their trust in a man who had now stolen from them. The police were kind but they also had a weary air. They had seen it all before and they would no doubt see it again in the future.

When the police spoke to them again, they said that a large number of people had been caught up in Martin Cole's fake investment scheme. It would be a complicated case because of the number of victims and the large sums involved. The good news was that they had traced the conman to Spain and they were liaising with the police there to bring him back. The bad news came later when they confirmed Eve and Frank's worst fears. All of the money had gone.

Behind every successful man is a determined woman. Frank had tweaked the saying to suit him and Eve. She was determined. She was the driving force. Early in their marriage, it had become apparent that they would never have a family and so Eve had devoted herself to making a success of the business. She could negotiate a better price, pick a winning product, and berate an errant member of staff. Frank was comfortable with his role as the figurehead of the company preferring the softly, softly approach to sales and staff management.

Frank had been a handsome dapper man when Eve met him. He was shorter than average but with her only being five foot two, that was not an issue. He had wanted a family as much as Eve had but they refused to be melancholy about their lack of success and refocused their energy. Twenty-five years after their wedding, Eve still saw the handsome man she loved. Yes, he was a bit greyer and his hair had receded and, yes, he had grown a little thicker round the middle, but he was still the love of her life.

***

As the dust settled after the discovery and the extent of their losses was realised, it was Eve who fought like a lioness to try and save the business. Frank was proud of his wife and never underestimated the massive contribution she had made to the success of their business. After her initial shock, she had come out fighting, working and reworking the figures to see if they could hold onto their livelihood, but Frank had already given in.

Frank admired his wife, but had accepted that her efforts were futile long before they finally closed it down. Eve, too, knew that she was fighting a losing battle, but hoped that Frank would be galvanised into action if she kept on trying. Instead, he slowly shut down with the last light blinking out as he lay in a hospital bed amidst a tangle of tubes and wires. He suffered a heart attack, collapsing at home, never regaining consciousness.

The worry and the shock made him feel ill. He didn't want to burden Eve with another problem so he suffered in silence. His heart had broken as he had to tell his loyal staff that their jobs and the business were gone. He got up each morning after the final closure and carried on the pretence that everything would be okay and that life would go back to normal.

After the business closed, Eve noticed that Frank was depressed, but that wasn't surprising given the circumstances. He moved more slowly and he didn't even want to go out and play golf. Frank had always been a stoic and he wouldn't complain but she was beginning to worry about him. The last few days he had been getting up later and he had looked pale and listless. As he came down the stairs he looked positively ashen.

On his last day, Frank found it extremely difficult to motivate himself to get out of bed. He felt incredibly tired and somewhat short of breath.

He didn't shower; he just put on the clothes that he had been wearing the day before and made his way downstairs. He felt an ominous tightening across his chest and pain in his arm as he collapsed to the floor. The look of shock on his wife's face was the last thing he saw.

What had Eve felt after Frank had died, she wondered? There was grief but the overwhelming feeling was anger. She was angry at Martin Cole for causing them so much misery and she was angry at Frank for giving up and dying. She was filled with a rage which made her, for a while, worry for her own sanity. She had felt murderous then when she thought of Martin Cole, and she still did. The rage she felt now though was a different thing entirely. It was a cold, hard, and determined steel that stiffened her spine and made her quite capable of killing someone.

Meeting Dorothea and Penny had been the one good thing to come out of the whole sorry episode. They met and were immediately drawn together in their anguish. They could talk to each other and truly empathise. Eve compressed her out of control anger into a solid core of hate, which would be directed only at those who were deserving of it. From their first meeting, the others watched Eve struggle to control her fury. They had no doubt she would kill without hesitation when the time came.

Her doctor worried about Eve too. She barely ate or slept in the months after Frank's death. He recommended that she undergo some sort of therapy to help her cope with the trauma of what had happened. This was not an option for Eve. She lived on the hate. She was fuelled by it. Having therapy might take the emotion away and she didn't want to give it up. She was sure that there would come a time when she would need it.

Each night before she went to bed, Eve looked through photos of her and Frank in happier times: on holiday, in front of their new warehouse, meeting the mayor at a business function, and, finally, at their wedding. Where others may have tried to forgive and forget, Eve stoked the fire. She had no children, no husband. and no business to focus on and she needed a cause. This new enterprise would give her a real life, not just an existence and, who knows, she might even enjoy it.

Chapter 6

"DNA is the big one," commented Dorothea. "The trouble is if you run around town buying coveralls and masks, it's a bit of a giveaway, the same goes for buying through the internet."

Penny gave the problem some thought and then raised her hand in a eureka moment. "I have a sewing machine. I'm sure I could run something up which would cover Eve from head to foot."

"Perhaps you could knit a balaclava too?" Dorothea enquired with a hint of sarcasm.

The sarcasm was lost on Penny who said, "Yes, of course."

The women found a tape measure and Eve was comprehensively appraised, every possible measurement recorded. The garment that Penny was making would cover Eve from head to foot, incorporating a hood to keep her hair from contaminating the scene of any murder.

"What material are you going to use?" Eve asked.

"I'll find something at home; I've got lots of fabric," Penny replied. Eve would later wish she had insisted on more input into the design.

Dorothea's house became the headquarters of their operation as it was halfway between the homes of the others. She put the kettle on again to make another pot of tea. Discussions like this had been going on for the last couple of weeks and progress was being made. They brainstormed for hours over the problem of tracing their future victims. The women finally agreed that in this computer age they would have to make use of the internet. Dorothea had a tablet computer, an unwanted gift from one of her sons, which would be used for the searches. One of them could sit in a cafe which had free wi-fi and find the information they needed. The tablet would be kept in a safe place but was small enough for them to destroy or dispose of should the need arise.

The love rat conman from the article, Simon Butler, who was a serial offender, had been provisionally earmarked as the first victim.

"We keep talking about the victim and murder but I think we should use other words in case we are out anywhere and we're overheard," Penny said.

Eve thought that was a good idea. "I suggest something to do with cooking. It's something we talk about all the time."

"You talk about it," laughed Penny. "I endure it."

Penny may have been married to a man who ran a catering business but that had not affected her inability to cook anything other than a basic meal.

Dorothea smiled, “We’ll keep it simple then. We won’t use any words associated with cordon bleu.”

Much hilarity ensued over the next half hour as they considered words such as toast (too obvious), stuffing (this just produced uncontrollable laughter), and baked, steamed, and boiled. They decided to call the victim “the dinner party guest” and then they could talk about when they got to serve him dessert, his just desserts, this was not entirely accurate Dorothea pointed out pedantically

“It should be just deserts with one s.”

Always a stickler for correct grammar and spelling, she had been a teacher, Dorothea needed to inform her friends of their error. The, well known, saying had been altered, through common usage, over time. It was important to her to make the point about its original form. Not that it mattered to Eve and Penny who just shrugged and carried on.

It was a bit corny but the ladies liked it. They tried it out in various forms. "The dinner party guest is going to be at home this weekend."

"We've served the guest dessert and we've cleaned up afterwards," Eve added

"There'll be no cheese and biscuits for the guest; he's taken more than his fair share," Penny grinned as she said, "It was his last supper."

They found Simon Butler's address. He lived in a town about fifty miles from theirs and now they were planning surveillance.

"We'll have to drive there and park well away from his home and then go the rest of the way on foot."

Penny bought a number of cheap wigs from a small shop in their home town. She was the first to admit that she was the type of woman who was practically invisible to the majority of the population. She was five foot five inches, average height, a size 16, just above average, with light brown hair. When she bought the wigs, the woman in the shop barely looked at her and Penny did not engage her in conversation or offer a reason for her purchase. There was a brief thank you before she drifted out of the shop. Of course, they had established that there was no CCTV in the place and, as she left, Penny transferred her goods to a differently branded plastic bag. If she was caught on camera further up the road, it would not be apparent where she had been.

The wigs and hats and other clothes, which they had bought from charity shops, would be used when they were in the vicinity of the dinner guest's home. The items they had bought included a red hooded top and a large brown anorak.

"I'm going to wash all those things before we wear them. Maybe I'll wash them twice," Penny was holding the coat at arm's length with a grimace on her face.

They would see if Simon had a routine and when his neighbours were around as well. How busy was the street, were there any security lights, and was it covered by the irksome CCTV? Most important of all was how they could gain access to his house.

Simon Butler lived on a fairly quiet street. His was a rather shabby rented semi-detached house. The front door did not look particularly robust but the chances of Eve kicking it in were slim. The neighbours were mostly young and seemed uninterested in anything that was happening outside of their own homes.

On a, late night, foray, Eve crept round the side of the house. She was actually out in the field, approaching the guest's house. Finally, a chance to put into practice, that which they had talked about for so long. No lights came on and the back garden was pitch black, so far so good. In preparation for getting into the house, Eve had been honing her lock picking skills. She didn't have the professional equipment but trawled through old crime shows freezing the screen when lock picks were shown and examining them carefully. It was amazing what you could fashion from hair pins and household detritus.

Eve would be covered from head to foot in Penny's homemade coverall. When Penny had produced it from a carrier bag with a flourish, the other two ladies were dumbfounded. It was made from a pair of old curtains. The material was green with darker green leaves embossed on it. Eve had hoped it would have something of the superhero look about it, not something of the garden centre. Underneath what was essentially a large romper suit, Eve would wear an old pair of trainers which had belonged to one of Dorothea's sons. Should any footprints be left, they would indicate that the killer wore a size nine. She would be wearing gloves, of course, and would be armed with a kitchen knife, sharpened to give it a lethal edge.

There were elaborate arrangements in place to supply an alibi. Dorothea would remain at home with Penny and they would record a number of programmes for Eve to watch later so that if asked they could describe in detail what they had watched that evening. They would make telephone calls from Eve's house using her mobile phone and use their mobile phones to call their children to show where they, allegedly, were. They would swear that they were all together should they be questioned.

Chapter 7

Royston Randall, Dorothea's husband, was the pride of his family. He climbed to the top of the ladder from humble beginnings and his wife, two sons, and his family back in Trinidad constantly sang his praises. They were contacted by the police and informed that Martin Cole, to whom they had entrusted their life savings, had gone missing. Over the next couple of weeks, it became increasingly certain that their money had gone missing too.

Dorothea and her husband were religious people who attended their local Baptist church every Sunday. They also supported the church by volunteering to help at fund raisers and events to help the community. They had faith in God and they had faith in their fellow man. Royston could not believe that they had been cheated by Martin Cole. He was ashamed that he had been duped and his belief in a benevolent God was sorely tested. He had fallen from his pedestal, successful businessman, community leader, and respected father, with a crash.

Over and over again, the couple asked why them. It was two months after the news first broke that Royston was diagnosed with prostate cancer. Dorothea had said, when the con was revealed, that they were being tested and that God would help them through this tough time. The cancer news on top of everything else made her begin to doubt the power of prayer. The church congregation would inform her every Sunday how they were praying for Royston but, when he died two months later, she knew that God had abandoned her. If, that was, He was actually there at all. She went to the funeral and, after that, she never returned to the church, physically or mentally, again.

Royston was a big man in height and in his standing in the community. He was a keen cricketer when he was young but had loved all other sport as well. Dorothea first saw him at a cricket match. He looked so good in his whites and, when he leapt athletically to catch a tricky ball, he caught her heart too. He was always the first to volunteer for things that were organized by the church, coaching the under elevens football team or selling raffle tickets or cajoling local businesses into sponsoring events. When it was revealed they had been the victims of a conman, his overwhelming emotion was shame. So many people looked up to him and respected his counsel. Not just his family, the members of his parish too.

He knew that pride was a sin, but Royston felt that his had been badly damaged. He went to church and listened to the commiserations of the congregation but were some of them a little pleased to see him brought low? Jealousy was a sin too but those around him had displayed signs of it and now they were reveling in his ruin. The prostate cancer diagnosis that had followed so soon after the shock of losing their money broke him. He knew that his wife would be looked after by the company for who he worked and that his sons were successful and happy. He lay back and waited to die.

The chemotherapy was draining, and the effects made him feel undignified. Despite the grim health diagnosis, pride wrought the most damage on him. Now that he had been humbled, he could not get back up. His marvelous wife Dorothea entreated him every day to fight for his life. She was strong and she was good. She also had faith and still had the respect of the congregation which would carry her through after he was gone. He was ready to meet his Lord.

The Pastor called at her house a few weeks after the funeral and she listened to his words and went through the charade of praying with him but she no longer believed. Her heart was full of pain and betrayal. She would bump into people from the congregation from time to time and they would tell her she was in their prayers but she just found it more and more irritating. She seriously considered punching one overly pious acquaintance when they had mentioned that it was all part of God's plan.

Their two sons drifted away from the church after they had left home many years before. Both of them were strong, tall, and athletic. This was particularly so of Robert who won a scholarship to an American college where he met his future wife and settled. She had two grandchildren in America, and she adored them from a distance. Thank goodness for computers that allowed her to speak to them and see them on a regular basis. Malcolm, her younger son, attended university in England and was a qualified lawyer practicing with a firm in the city. Robert was abroad and Malcolm was busy with his life in the city so she had sold their large family home and moved near to her new friends Eve and Penny.

Her friendship with the others had been a major factor in her, still only partial, recovery from her double tragedy. The loss of the money had seemed such a big thing at the time but, compared to the loss of Royston, it was a mere irritation. Eve had appeared strong but was brittle underneath and Penny was barely coping when they met. She had needed a reason to carry on so she took on the care of these two ladies and, together, they found the strength to rebuild their lives.

Dorothea sat through the trial and saw the justice handed down to Martin Cole. She was now convinced, however, that there would be no judgment in any afterlife. If their little trio could mete out some form of retribution on the fraudsters of the world, then she was all for it. She had never been able to stand the sight of blood though and this had dictated her role as planner rather than doer.

Dorothea had a good brain on her. She had taught English but retired at fifty-five. She kept her mind active with crossword puzzles and she read constantly. Solving the problems that were apparent when they embarked on this course would be a whole new challenge. It would be a great achievement to plan the perfect murder.

She did wonder what her sons would make of the latest direction her life was taking. They would never believe that she was part of a murder plot. An integral part of a murder plot, a lot of the planning had been down to her. Eve quipped that at least they would have a lawyer if things did not work out as planned. Dorothea pointed out that her son specialized in employment law so he would be of limited use.

Around the table in the kitchen, the ladies put the finishing touches to their plot and ran through what they hoped would be the sequence of events. They didn't talk about what may happen if they got caught. After what they had been through, it was not worth worrying about. There was almost a festive atmosphere as they raised a glass of wine in a toast to the end of the dinner party guest.

Chapter 8

Eve set off in Penny's car around five in the afternoon. It would take just over an hour to reach her destination, but the crime would not be committed until at least eight o'clock. They did not think that the police would be searching through CCTV of vehicles entering the town two hours before the crime. Penny's car was a silver Ford Fiesta of which there were thousands on the road. The number plates had been altered with the application of insulating tape which had turned the F into an E and the L into an E also. The P had become a B. Eve would drive into the town using one route and exit using another.

As Eve walked down the main road toward Simon Butler's street, she was wearing a long blonde wig, jeans, a blue jacket, and heels. She looked down at an old mobile phone, which was not functional, as she walked to avoid giving a good shot of her face to any CCTV cameras. She turned into the street which was deserted and walked slowly past the dinner party guest's house. A light was on in the front room and there was the flicker of a television. She casually strolled down the side of the house and stood for a moment in the dark back garden listening for any movement.

The only thing Eve could hear was distant traffic and the noise of Simon's television. Good, he liked it turned up loud. Eve pulled off her wig and threw it into the bag she was carrying with her. The trainers came out of the bag and were put on, followed by the homemade onesie which covered the trainers as well. The homemade mask with the elastic loops hooked over her ears, a pair of goggles were donned, and finally the gloves. Her face was almost completely covered which would avoid her having to leave smeared in blood. Not a good look for strolling through town.

The makeshift lock picks were produced and, most importantly, the knife.

On her knees in front of the back door, Eve prepared herself for what she thought would be a tricky part of her job. On a whim, she tested the handle and found that the door was unlocked. She had to cover her mouth with her hands to stop herself laughing out loud. Right, into the kitchen and then make her way through to the front room. The door was open and she could see the top of Simon's head over the back of the chair. The moment was here and Eve could barely contain her excitement. He hadn't heard her approach and she gripped the knife ready to plunge it into his jugular vein.

***

In the morning, Simon was due to see his solicitor. He had been released from prison six months before having served a sentence for the fraud on Patricia, but inevitably he had tried his luck again and was now facing new charges. He would have to shower and find something clean to wear which was a real drag. When he was "working," he had to keep himself together to impress his victims but when he was between jobs he liked to chill out. If he didn't have to leave the house, he didn't bother to get dressed. He had tried to charm his solicitor Angela but the flattery, the wide-eyed innocence, and the tales of his terrible childhood had cut no ice with her. Oh well, not all of the women he met took to him, but there were enough that did and he made a good living from them. He had insisted on pleading not guilty again in the hope that luck would be on his side. Angela had doubted his chances of getting off but had to follow her client's instructions and was trying to find something positive to say about him.

He accepted his latest arrest as an occupational hazard. It was not his first rodeo. The judge would not be able to give him a lengthy sentence because of the guidelines and he would be out and working again in no time. He would learn from his mistakes though. Nest time he should work the con over a longer period. He had been in too much of a hurry to get money out of the last one and pushing too hard had made her crack. That had led to his downfall. These crazy old bitches wouldn't be allowed to get the better of him again.

The story about Simon's terrible childhood had been complete fiction. He had been the only child of loving parents. They had cosseted and flattered their son and smothered him with affection. If he wanted something, he simply had to ask. The unfortunate effect of his upbringing was that he never learnt the value of hard work. When his father died, his mother had become very needy. He had made money in the easiest way he could find. He had a real talent for getting the clothes off women's backs and the money out of their purses.

When times were hard, he went home to his mother and pleaded poverty to get a hand out. Simon eventually used up his goodwill with his mother and she told him that no more money would be forthcoming. He didn't really see his mother after that as she was of no further use.

Simon was watching some reality show which featured, in his words, fit birds. He was totally absorbed in a lovers' tiff enacted by the good-looking cast members. The girl was crying now and begging the man not to leave. It was a scenario in which he had had a starring role on many an occasion. Was that movement behind him? Who would be in his house? Twisting around he was most surprised by what he saw. A small person wearing a green leaf patterned coverall and goggles. Eve plunged the knife into his neck and watched the blood spray from the wound. The dinner guest made a slight gurgling sound and then he was dead.

***

Well that had been quite simple. Eve knew that she was lucky though. Simon Butler had been sitting down with his back to her and she had the element of surprise. When the moment came, she did not hesitate. She had consulted a medical manual that Penny's husband owned, so she knew exactly where to aim her blow. God, this room was a mess. She would have to be careful negotiating her way out without disturbing anything.

Simon Butler had been eating a bowl of cereal in his chair in a dressing gown and slippers. The bowl was now on the floor but strangely he was still holding the spoon. How pathetic he looked. Was this really the man who had charmed so many women out of their money and broken their hearts? Well, he wouldn't be doing it again. Eve couldn't help pausing for a second to take in the scene. She wanted to remember this moment and describe the details to her friends.

Rousing herself, Eve went back through the house and out of the back door. Having been behind her victim she had not been sprayed with as much blood as she expected and didn't appear to leave any trail. She had done it. Simon Butler was dead, and it looked like she was going to get away with it. A smile was spreading onto her face. Outside, she removed the green romper suit and put it and the knife in a plastic bag. She then put on a short brown wig and a pair of glasses and a red hoodie. Finally, she arranged her goods into a differently branded plastic bag than the one she had walked in with and made her way to the front of the house.

The street was still deserted, and Eve left in the opposite direction and zigzagged through the back streets rejoining the main road at a different place from where she had left it. On CCTV, she would be a brunette in a red hoodie carrying a supermarket carrier bag and wearing trainers. The trainers were a few sizes too big and difficult to walk in but it was good because it made her walk slowly when the temptation was to hurry. When she arrived back at the car, she relaxed and once inside, she grinned at herself in the rear-view mirror. Now for a steady drive back to Dorothea's.

It was nine thirty when Eve got back and after removing the tape from the number plates she went inside to her anxious friends.

"We are very pleased to see you. How did it go?"

Eve was beaming so they knew it must have gone well. "The dinner party guest is no more," she declared solemnly.

The three women jumped up and down like excited schoolgirls hugging each other and laughing. Penny wanted to know all the gory details.

"Not too gory please," Dorothea begged.

The unlocked door, the gurgling sound, and the spoon were all included in Eve's description. She managed to get around the back of the house with relative ease, the street was deserted. When she found the back door unlocked, she had struggled to remain quiet, tempted to laugh out loud. The guest had his back to her watching one of those reality shows. It was only at the last moment that he turned his head towards her.

"You know when people say they did a double take, well that is what he did. He couldn't quite believe what was coming at him. He was puzzled and then he smiled, like it was a joke. He soon found out that it wasn't." Eve finished by saying how pathetic he had looked, half dressed, still clutching his spoon in the filthy room.

"He was eating cereal at eight o'clock at night!" Penny relished the information and, although she shivered a couple of times, Dorothea was rapt too.

"We need to refine the process a bit, I think," commented Eve. "He was sat in a chair and an easy target but what if he had been on his feet and able to overpower me. We focused so much on getting in and out that we forgot about the actual deed."

Dorothea pointed out that people would be less likely to "have a go" if they were looking down the barrel of a gun. "You wouldn't need to use it, just wave it around. That's if we can get hold of one, of course."

Penny announced, "I've got a gun."

After getting over the Penny's startling statement, the ladies arranged to meet the next evening to discuss the operation in minute detail and talk through the ramifications of taking a gun. They wanted a full debrief so that they could make any necessary tweaks. For now, they were too excited, and they cracked open a bottle of bubbly to celebrate their first success.

"Here's to the first one. Let's find victim, sorry, dinner guest number two."

Chapter 9

Detective Inspector Mike Nash pulled up to the once quiet street where the body had been found to discover two police cars and a crowd of ghoulish onlookers. The press would no doubt be arriving soon as well. A young police officer who was standing guard directed him to the rear of the property where three other officers had congregated.

He uttered the words which had been repeated so many times both in real life and in fiction. "What have we got then?"

The victim was a man called Simon Butler he was informed. "Simon Butler? I know that name."

The officer confirmed that he was on bail for fraud and that he had a string of previous convictions. Simon had been due at his solicitor's on Monday morning, but had not arrived. Following attempts to reach him by phone, the solicitor, Angela Frost, had driven past his house and seen the car in the drive. Simon was not inclined to do much and didn't even walk the three hundred yards to the local shop, she informed them, and so she knew he must be at home. She had hammered on the door and eventually peered through the window where she was met by the gruesome sight of his corpse.

Angela was a bit shaken up by the discovery, but decided she wasn't particularly troubled that her client had met his demise. She hated having to defend people like Simon Butler, but someone had to do it. She thought about how he had tried his charm on her and then his sob story, but there was no excuse for what he had done. He had wanted to plead not guilty, which was ridiculous and she advised against it, but he insisted. Their meeting that day was to try again to find any mitigating circumstances she could raise during the trial.

"Have you been in the house?" Mike asked one of the officers.

"Just a quick walk through to check he was dead and that no one else was present. The back door was unlocked. The scene of crime people should be on their way."

Mike was itching to look at the scene, but decided he was not going to go into the house until forensics had done their bit. Checks had been done and he didn't want to disturb the scene any more. They waited for the forensic team to arrive and Mike ran through in his mind what a nightmare case this could turn into if they didn't turn up anything. The trouble with the murder of a man like Simon was that so many people wanted him dead.

The news cameras had arrived and caught the scene of crime officers entering the house in their white coveralls. Mike waited an inordinately long time before donning foot covers and gloves and being allowed into Simon's house. He wouldn't have to wait for the medical examiner's report for the cause of death. A jagged hole in the neck of the victim explained all. He would have bled out within minutes but would have been unconscious almost immediately as his blood pressure rapidly dropped. It was a surgical strike, not a frenzy of stabs that you often see when a murder is personal, but he would not form any solid conclusions at this early stage.

A junior detective, Adam Ashton, arrived and was taking notes as he followed Mike around from room to room. The solicitor's description of Simon as a lazy slob was most accurate. The house was filthy and the smell of food, mainly from takeaways, congealing on plates, and dirty laundry had been joined by the aroma of Simon's corpse.

"I don't know if we'll catch the killer but we might catch salmonella," joked one of the older officers.

Mike studied the corpse and noted the spoon still clutched in his hand and found it hard to motivate himself to find the killer of this revolting man. The forensics team was still collecting items from the house which may contain DNA and the room was speckled with powder that had been dusted on surfaces in an effort to recover any fingerprints. It was his job to find the killer though and, being satisfied that no further information could be gleaned from the scene at this time, he took a slightly green looking Adam back to police headquarters. On the way out, he was asked to say something to the assembled television news cameras, and he gave the usual response about no details being released at that time and that it was an ongoing investigation. Mike also made an appeal for anyone that had seen anything to come forward. Back at the station, he started the paperwork for the new case and began looking at the long list of people the deceased had conned over the years.

The young detective, Adam, who was assigned to assist Mike, was still fairly new to the role. He gained a degree at university and then joined the force on the fast track programme. He excelled and had been working as a detective for six months. Working on a homicide case was exciting and terrifying at the same time. Adam was twenty-six but still looked like an eighteen-year-old. He had a slight build and light brown downy hair. Mike was wondering how he would get on in an interrogation. He was probably not going to be able to play the bad cop.

***

On the six o'clock news, pictures were transmitted live from outside the house where the murder had taken place. The reporter intoned gravely, but somewhat breathlessly, that the victim, named locally as Simon Butler, had been discovered by his solicitor when he failed to attend an appointment. There was the usual police appeal for information from a rather handsome detective and then the details of Simon's many indiscretions were given and the reporter signed off and handed back to the studio. He hadn't smiled at the end of his piece but he hadn't looked very bothered either.

Dorothea, Penny, and Eve watched the report and high fived each other afterwards. Eve turned to the others and said, "If I am arrested, I wouldn't mind him taking down my particulars."

After the giggling stopped, they convened in the kitchen and began a full debrief. They felt like celebrities having their handiwork appear on television. It was a pity that they couldn't show off to anyone else.

***

It was disturbing to read the stories of the women Simon Butler had conned over the years. Mike rubbed at his temples as his head began to ache from the relentless grim reports he was reading. The conman had chosen his prey carefully, concentrating on women in their forties from affluent areas. Presumably, he could clean up quite well because a stream of women had agreed to go out with him. Before long they had fallen for his lies and were handing over their cash.

It amazed Mike that so many people had been fooled by Simon Butler but he had only seen the corpse. When he spoke to officers from the fraud department, they talked of a charming credible man who one would be happy to meet for a drink and call a friend. He thought it was unlikely that one of these women had killed him. The manner of the attack indicated a well-planned murder. Women often committed murder when emotional. A spur of the moment act. Simon Butler sitting in his dressing gown eating a bowl of cereal wasn't likely to arouse any emotion other than revulsion.

The list of suspects was growing by the minute. The women who had been wronged were now being joined by their relatives and friends, who may have taken it on themselves or been convinced to exact revenge. Over the next few weeks, the news from forensics was depressingly bad. No fingerprints, shoe prints, or DNA. No murder weapon had been found and a canvassing of the area had provided no witnesses. CCTV was now being searched for cars and people in the vicinity on the Sunday evening between eight and midnight when the murder was thought to have taken place.

A seemingly endless trail of people appeared at the station to be questioned. Adam asked if interviewing all these people was a waste of time considering they had no physical evidence. Mike was an experienced officer and said it was worthwhile.

"We interview all these people to see their reactions. If someone is involved, they are often evasive or over confident. Often, they tell a story and then details change, so we look out for inconsistencies as they can indicate guilt. It's a sense that you develop when you've done a few of these enquiries. If we fancy someone for it then we try to build a case."

The reactions of the women being interviewed were interesting. Some were resigned, they were not surprised, some were gleeful and, startlingly, some were heartbroken. Adam made a fair few trips to get tea and tissues for the grieving victims. A mountain of paperwork was being accumulated and every syllable of every statement was pored over in an effort to detect some sort of clue. They were being buried under the amount of mobile phone data they had collected but no one on their list of suspects had been found to be in the vicinity of Simon's home on the night in question.

Alibis were verified and the criminal records of suspects were checked but nothing had come to light. Mike had sleepless nights about the lack of evidence and how this would affect his arrest record. He wasn't thinking about getting justice for Simon Butler or his mother who had been somewhat indifferent on being given the sad news.

Hours were spent trawling through the CCTV pictures for the night of Simon's murder.

People were seen leaving the high street and walking down the road where the victim lived but no one had been seen coming back out again a few minutes later. There were no cars that appeared in the area at the time that aroused suspicion either. The search widened to include more streets and motorways in and out of the area but, again, they drew a blank.

Over time, other crimes were committed, and priorities changed, and the case was relegated to the back burner. A reminder to review the evidence popped onto Mike's computer screen at regular intervals but he would just move it to another week. Unless somebody came forward with information, they had hit a dead end. It was difficult to motivate the public when the victim was a habitual criminal, so a further television appeal had been deemed a waste of resources.

Even the newspapers, which had been so desperate to reveal the gritty details of Simon

Butler's life and death, could not be bothered to return to the story after a few weeks. Some of the women who had been conned had reaped a financial reward from selling their stories in the wake of the murder, but now the media had moved on to new, more sympathetic, victims.

Chapter 10

After the first murder, the friends went through the whole thing step by step to see what had worked well and what could be refined. The biggest problem, as Eve had pointed out, would be what would happen if someone was in a position to fight back. The revelation that Penny owned a gun had provoked a discussion. Eve didn't want to use it as the murder weapon, mainly because it would make too much noise and therefore attract attention. Dorothea proposed that Eve could point it at someone, if they were being uncooperative, and force them to kneel on the floor. She could then move behind them and use the knife.

They all agreed that the disguises had worked well and that they would need to mix and match their outfits regularly to throw the police off the scent. They had to treat the surveillance like a proper job. When they had reported their observations back to Dorothea of an evening, Penny and Eve had given details, but had also admitted becoming distracted at times. There would be no more wandering off to shop or, if Penny and Eve were together, no discussing or critiquing what someone was wearing.

"It's hard not to comment on some of the crimes against fashion." said Eve. "Sometimes we need a break from thinking about murder."

"Yes. We chat to pass the time. We can't talk about killing all the time, other topics come up. Point taken though, more watching less gossip." Penny said.

They both assumed a suitably chastised demeanour when Dorothea glared at them before starting to laugh.

The ladies were now planning their next operation. They had taken to buying those weekly magazines that featured true life stories so that they could search for a fraudster to focus on. They didn't rush into a decision as they wanted to make sure the next subject was worthy of their attention. Love rats, as the men were dubbed by the press, filled the pages of most of the publications. They weren't sure in some cases who was guiltier, the man who led the woman on or the woman who allowed it to happen. There were a few women who had conned people. They tended to steal from companies they were working for or from people they were supposed to be caring for. As despicable as those crimes were, they didn't really want to kill a woman. The waiting paid off when they found the story of Eddie Stringer.

This villain had run a boiler room scam. His small outfit had targeted elderly people on the phone convincing them that they could reap large rewards by investing in shares in companies that simply didn't exist. Sums of money were paid and bogus certificates were issued and the money was spent on small bonuses for the unscrupulous staff and large luxuries for the despicable Eddie.

Eddie was leading a life of luxury with the proceeds of his crimes. He lived in a big house which had a swimming pool and a sauna. His semi famous girlfriend wandered around in bikinis or lingerie which he found delightful. When Justine had been at the peak of her career, she was photographed either in the nude or with very little on. She seemed to have developed an aversion to wearing a lot of clothes, it was noted.

There were a couple of nice cars in the garage and Eddie also had a games room which was his pride and joy. For him, games were something one played on a computer whilst sat in a comfy chair with a drink on hand. The large screen on the wall enabled him to immerse himself in the games.

Many of the victims were not only elderly but were easily confused too. By targeting a certain age group, Eddie had been able to carry on his enterprise for some time before he was caught. A relative of one of the sufferers became suspicious when he saw a large amount leave his grandmother's account. She was not entirely sure what the money was for but had been sent a certificate. It didn't take long to establish that the company, in which she supposedly owned shares, was bogus. He went to the police.

One of the pictures in the magazine was of an elderly couple who were sat holding hands on a flowery sofa. Their expressions were of sadness tinged with bewilderment. Mr. and Mrs. Brook had received a phone call from one of Eddie's sales people and been told about the marvelous opportunity for which they had been selected. An up and coming company specializing in new computer technology was to be floated on the stock exchange and they could buy the shares at a very low price and then sell them a few weeks later for a profit. They may even double their money.

The couple asked for something in writing and a letter with the heading Edwards & Co. Stockbrokers had arrived. It stated how pleased they were to have a chance to help them make money and how time was of the essence if they wished to take up this once in a lifetime offer. It directed them to the company website which featured several testimonials from satisfied customers. They wrote a cheque and sent it off and a few days later a share certificate arrived together with a letter advising them that they would be contacted when the market was right for them to sell. They never heard from the stockbrokers again. The company did not exist. The article noted that Mr. and Mrs. Brook cried when they talked of losing their life savings but that they agreed to the interview in order to warn other people not to get scammed like they had.

Penny studied the other picture in the magazine of the balding overweight man with the colourful shirt straining over his enormous belly and the huge gold bracelet dangling from his wrist. Eddie Stringer was a walking cliché of a conman.

"If you can catch him sitting down it'll be no problem. It would probably take him half an hour to get out of his chair," she observed.

"I have a strange urge to discover him in a hot tub and finish him off there." Eve was gazing wistfully across the room.

"He is definitely the type of man that would have a hot tub," Dorothea said. "And he would be wearing a tiny brief swimming costume in it or a thong." A chorus of "eeews" ensued.

"Okay, let's get to work now that our new guest had been identified," Dorothea said.

"Penny, are you okay to take the tablet to the café and look him up?" She nodded her agreement and asked Eve if she needed a new coverall.

"No, the one I've got is fine. It has a certain shock value when viewed by the guest that is quite satisfying. It must be like being attacked by a potted plant."

Research revealed that Eddie had been living with a "model" who had packed her designer clothes and departed the minute he was caught and the money dried up. He too was conveniently local as he was now living in a commuter belt town only twenty miles away from them since his release from prison. He lived in a flat in a small block in a nice part of the town. He must have kept a stash of money somewhere to be able to afford that.

The wigs were taken out of storage and a new surveillance operation was set up. Dorothea had decided that she would like to take part in the field work and would wear a grey wig and walk around the area stooped over a tartan shopping trolley like an elderly lady. She liked her new role and she soon reported that Eddie left his house only occasionally. He went to the bookies or the local shop or to the pub. He was a creature of habit and could be relied upon to be wobbling home from the pub, up a path that was next to a park, after closing time on a Friday night. The path was unlit and therefore not used much after dark, making it the ideal place for an ambush. Eve could emerge from the foliage, where she would be perfectly camouflaged, deliver the fatal blow, and then disappear back into the undergrowth where her bag of alternative clothes would be waiting. She was quite looking forward to it.

There were, of course, obstacles to be overcome. Getting out of the park late at night without registering on CCTV was the main problem. What woman would choose to be in that area late at night alone? Eve had an idea.

"I'm small and flat chested. I'm sure that I could pass for a teenage boy. I'll wear a beanie hat and travel through the park on a scooter with a rucksack on my back."

"Some of those scooters fold up so you will be able to carry it in a bag down the path and then exit the park as a boy on wheels" Penny advised. "My grandson Dylan has been asking for one for ages, so I'll get one for his birthday."

"Will it be alright giving him a gift that has been used in a murder?" Dorothea asked.

“Its only transport, I’m not going to club him around the head with it.” Eve pointed out.

“Quite.” Penny couldn’t see a problem.

As this murder would be taking place outside, there would be no worries about getting in and out of a block of flats. Eddie’s home had one of those entry systems where you identified yourself before being buzzed in and they had puzzled over what reason they could give that would make him admit Eve. The weekly wobble from the pub solved the problem.

A fold up scooter was purchased with cash from a large toy shop chain on a busy Saturday. It was an extra precaution which they thought was redundant really, as Penny was going to give the scooter to her grandson after the murder. She was just a granny buying a birthday present. The packaging of the scooter was removed carefully and stored because it would have to be wrapped up again afterwards. Eve practiced folding and unfolding the scooter ready for her somewhat unconventional getaway.

"Don't forget to slouch, teenagers always slouch," Dorothea coached Eve who was pushing the scooter and then riding up and down the lounge.

Penny had a fit of giggles and once she composed herself she enquired whether Eve should have a pair of those jeans on that "show half your arse."

"I'm not that kind of teenager." Eve replied prissily. "My mother won't let me out dressed like that."

Chapter 11

Penny had always thought of herself as ordinary and she was astonished that Derek had shown an interest in her when they met in their teens. She would often tell him that she was ordinary, and he would reply that he was ordinary too but together they were extraordinary. It was one of his favourite quips. At the time, Penny worked in a bank as a cashier and Derek was training to be a chef. A family friend asked Derek to cater for a party and the idea for their business was born.

It was a longstanding joke that Derek, a chef, was married to a woman that could just about boil an egg. She did contribute to the business though. She issued invoices and typed quotes and together they were a good team. The business grew and she gave up work at the bank and they bought a commercial building with a proper professional kitchen and the orders rolled in. They had two daughters, Kirsty and Laura, and life was good.

Her husband was always a worrier. He inspected every item that left the kitchen and constantly stood over his staff as they worked, often shooing them out of the way so that he could take over. Their profits would have been greater had he not rejected so many dishes that he thought were not up to standard. The rejected food usually found its way back to the family home where it was always met with delight. Derek's dishes were good even if he thought they were below par and it also meant that no one had to eat Penny's cooking.

A refit of the kitchen with new modern-day appliances had taken place shortly before the news of Martin Cole's disappearance was received. They had been planning on paying for the kitchen update with money from their investment. The money that was no longer there. Derek heard the news and pretty much stopped functioning from that moment on. He would go to work and sit in the office and leave his staff to their own devices.

They managed, somehow, to pay for the kitchen refit, but then struggled to pay for wages and provisions. On a Friday evening when he knew that the business could not carry on, a disconsolate Derek came home and slumped into his chair. He then announced that he was taking a walk to the corner shop and got up and left. The trip took fifteen minutes. After thirty minutes, Penny began to become concerned and after an hour, she was filled with dread. At the front door, Penny heard the sound of a car engine coming from the detached garage. She initially thought that he had driven to the shop and had just come home but then noticed that the garage door was closed.

The ordinary woman took just a moment to deduce what this meant. Penny ran to the garage, opened the door, and was met by a wall of exhaust. Her daughters had married and left home years before so she ran back into the empty house and stood in the hallway. Yes, the phone, she should phone someone. She dialed 999 and when the operator asked which service she required, she said send everyone. The police and ambulance were dispatched and Penny ran back to the garage where the smoke had now begun to clear and she was able to get to the car and open the door. Derek was sat in the seat looking like he had just dozed off. There was no pulse; he was dead.

***

Running a business was a burden for Derek. It was successful and Penny helped but as he lay in bed at night, Derek ran through all the things that he had to do the next day and the day after and so on until his head pounded. He saw the staff raise their eyebrows and heard their sighs when he found some slight fault with what they were doing. He wasn't going to change though. Why do a job at all if you didn't strive for perfection?

He was a man who lived on his nerves. He worried constantly about the business and his other big worry was his health. When Derek's head was aching, he thought he had a tumour. When his stomach growled, he assumed that it had to be some form of bowel disease. For some reason that Penny couldn't fathom, he was also overly fond of material possessions. He hated throwing anything away in the early years of their marriage but had become better over time.

The disappearance of Martin Cole and their money made the future seem hopeless. It didn't seem hopeless; it was hopeless. They would never be able to recover from the loss coming at the time that they had invested so much in new equipment. Derek never thought of trying to find a solution, he only thought about the terrible impact on him. He had a gun in his secret lock up garage and it constantly occupied his thoughts. He wanted to die and the only question remaining was how he would accomplish the task.

In the end, Derek could not pluck up the courage to shoot himself. Instead he chose to gas himself in his car. It would be like falling asleep, no blood or mess, only peace. As he became befuddled from the exhaust fumes, he did briefly think about Penny. He thought that she and the girls would be better off without him.

The police and ambulance men were very kind. Hot sweet tea was delivered to her as she sat wrapped in a blanket and somebody phoned her daughters who arrived as quickly as they could. The three women cried together sat on the sofa as the emergency crews carried on with their work. That night had been etched on her memory ever since. She would hear a siren and she would feel the goose bumps rise as she recalled the sight of her dead husband.

There was no mercy from the media when the story broke. Derek's death was linked to the loss of money to a Ponzi scheme and journalists plagued Penny for weeks afterwards. "How do you feel about your husband's death?" and other inane questions were fired at her whenever she left the house. They would not be happy, she felt, until she was caught sobbing for their cameras. Inevitably, a new more sensational story took precedence over her loss and she was left alone.

The mix of emotions that Penny felt veered between grief, guilt that had she should have gone into the garage sooner, and anger. He had left her alone to sort out the mess. Had he thought about her and what she would have to face when he had taken his life? Had he thought about their girls and grandchildren? Like Eve, she sold her beautiful home, paid off the creditors, and was now living in a tiny apartment.

The stigma of a suicide was an almost tangible thing. People she knew either whispered to her in hushed tones, or scuttled away in the opposite direction when she ran into them. Her grief transformed itself into something new. She found that she despised Derek. All those odd foibles, the hypochondria, and the hoarding were no longer faintly amusing. They were indications of Derek's true nature. He had been a coward.

Kirsty and Laura were good to her. Their childhood was carefree, and they had wanted for nothing so now they didn't mind supplementing their mother's meagre income, but she hated having to take their money. Kirsty had a son, Dylan, and Laura had a daughter, Katie. They should be spending their money on them, not on her.

The court case brought her into contact with Dorothea and Eve and they had been instrumental in helping their mother's recovery. Their circumstances were different, but they understood, more than anyone, what she was going through. Dorothea provided care and sympathy and Eve shared her resilience. Between them, they managed to survive what life had thrown at them.

Amongst her husband's effects, Penny found the title deed to a lock up garage about three miles from their old home. She had not known about it and went to look at it after a few months, nervously wondering what on earth was in there. It turned out to be storage for everything that, over the years, she had asked Derek to get rid of. He had always been a hoarder, but she thought that over time he had reformed. The place contained old toasters and radios and other electrical items. There were old clothes in carrier bags and boxes of books and magazines. A couple of broken chairs shared the space as well. The place was full to the rafters and seeing it made Penny angry again.

She visited the lock up regularly, gradually working through the piles of stuff in the hope that she would find something of value. Then she found the gun. It was stuffed in a shoebox, wrapped in an old silk scarf. She had no idea where the gun came from and she considered handing it in to the police. But she hadn't. Knowing the gun was in her apartment had been a burden and now it was a bonus.

Eve and Dorothea rebuilt Penny who had been close, at times, to following her husband. There were still days when she felt quite overwhelmed but now she could pick up the phone to someone who had experienced something very similar. They would make her laugh or tell her off and she would get through another day. Their crusade to rid the world of evil fraudsters was helping her recovery to no end. Sitting and brooding about the past had been replaced with positive action (for them).

Chapter 12

Disguised as an old lady, Dorothea was able to trundle her tartan trolley around the park, pausing every now and then as if to rest or catch her breath and get a good idea of its features. She drew a diagram, which had since been burnt, showing where Eve could gain access through gaps in the bushes to the path where the dinner guest would be. She also earmarked a large thicket that would provide cover when the green assassin had to change clothes and transform into a teenage boy.

The elaborate arrangement with the phone calls had been abandoned this time as the murder was to take place late at night and, they reasoned, they would not be using their phones at that time. It would be perfectly legitimate to claim that they were all tucked up in their own beds should they be questioned on their whereabouts. For this trip,

Eve would be taking Dorothea's car, a white Renault, which would be subject to the insulating tape alterations to the number plate.

Again, the timings of various activities were crucial and it was decided that Eve should walk down the path next to the park at around nine o'clock. A woman wouldn't want to be walking alone along the dark track any later than that. She would be carrying a bag and a jacket which would be folded round the scooter with the lining facing outwards. She would creep through to the park close to the thicket and, at an opportune moment, secrete herself inside to await the arrival of the guest.

As she drove Dorothea's car to the nearby town, Eve sang along to the radio. A sense of excitement was building and, once she had parked the car in a back street, she had to stop herself from skipping down the road to her destination. She was wearing a black curly wig and carrying a jacket and a carrier bag, which contained the rucksack she would don later. The path was deserted and she was able to enter the park and then the thicket between members of the public passing by.

Safely inside the thicket, there was plenty of time for preparation. Eve had to change into the green coverall, goggles and mask, but before she did that, she wanted to prepare herself mentally. Penny and Dorothea's words were in her ears as she replayed their advice.

"Don't rush. You can always walk away and try another time."

"Yes, we want to do the job, but its not worth it if you are caught."

Eve suppressed her excitement and made plans to be cautious in her approach and to ensure that the coast was clear before striking. Delivering the fatal blow was the easiest part of the whole thing, she thought. At eleven o'clock, she changed into her killing outfit and did a few bends and stretches to limber up. Eddie would be tottering past at eleven forty or thereabouts and she moved into place ten minutes before he was due.

Shortly after she had crouched in the bushes, she heard brisk footsteps on the path. That was definitely not the sound of Eddie approaching. She stayed perfectly still and watched a young man walk past. At the speed he was going, he would be well out of the way when the guest arrived. The time was eleven forty-two when the slow shuffling plod of an obese man echoed down the path. She could even hear his rasping breath. He tottered past her hiding place and she peered out in both directions, checking that no one else was around. To her relief, the path was clear and she closed in on her victim from behind with the knife in her hand.

***

He didn't know why he went to that pub every week. Eddie would sit in the corner ignored by the other customers and consume several large vodka and cokes. He went because he had no friends and nowhere else to go he supposed. All his friends and his girlfriend Justine had left after he had been caught. He was under no illusion about why Justine had been with him, his money, but the pros far outweighed the cons in that arrangement. Strutting into a club or restaurant with a beautiful minor celebrity on his arm was awesome. He had hoped some of his other friends would stick around. He was now painfully aware of how little they liked anything about him other than his wealth.

Some of his so-called mates gave evidence at his trial. How moral they had become in the wake of his arrest. They shook their heads and talked about how all those poor pensioners had lost their savings, the savings that they had helped him spend. Justine was the first to go. He was arrested in a dawn raid and, by the time he was released on bail, she had collected all her things and several of his more expensive possessions and gone. She was never a suspect as initial questioning soon revealed that she would never have been able to mastermind such a scheme. She would not be able to organise the proverbial booze up. When Eddie returned, there was no Justine and she hadn't even left a note.

It was a shame he had been caught. This latest scam had been his most profitable. He did sometimes feel a bit sorry for the people that he conned but soon got over it. Shopping for new gadgets always made him feel better. The police confiscated all the valuable stuff like cars, electronics, and jewellery but he had kept some cash hidden away and was now living quite comfortably off of that. The time in prison gave him time to think up a new scheme to make money.

As he walked home from the pub, Eddie cursed his former friends who were nowhere to be seen. The other customers in the bar avoided him as if he was plague ridden, so he sat alone when he was in there. He chatted to the girl who worked in the bookies but that was the nearest thing he had to a friend now. All that would change when he started making money again. Eddie knew now that he needed money not just to live but to buy companionship as well. If that Justine tried to crawl back, he would send her packing. On second thought, if she was suitably contrite, he might take her on again. He didn't want to cut off his nose to spite his face.

Eddie thought he heard something, and he turned to the side to be met with the sight of something small and green rapidly approaching. He saw the thing raise its arm and then he was stabbed in the neck. Eve stood back as Eddie crumpled to the floor blood gushing out of his neck. His eyes were still wide open in surprise as he died. She noted that he also made a gurgling sound but with a hint of wheeze.

***

There was no time for reflection after this murder. She was in a public place and had to move fast. Eve took a step and then glanced down to where she had left a large bloody footprint. The blood was only on one foot so she hopped to the bushes and, leaning against a tree, took off the green romper. What would the police think of that, one large footprint and then nothing else?

She would not be so well camouflaged on her trip back to the thicket, but the park was empty and she made it there without incident. Grab the bag, pull on the beanie hat, and change her trainers. She had barely been able to walk in the size nines and there was no way she could ride a scooter in them. The coverall and knife went into a plastic bag and then into the rucksack. She put on the jacket, assembled the scooter, and then emerged into the deserted park.

She rode her scooter to the park entrance which led to the main road and then trundled along the pavement. Eve paused before she got to the corner where a streetlight was glowing. In a pre-planned move, she got a mobile phone out of her pocket and was looking down studying it closely as she passed under the bright light. There would be no good view of her features on any CCTV camera.

Once around the corner, Eve relaxed a little and enjoyed whizzing along on her scooter ride back to the car. The scooter, rucksack, jacket, and beanie hat were put in the boot and Eve climbed into the car and flicked her fingers through her hair. The car was parked in the dark at the end of a street next to waste land and she was not observed. She took a deep breath and then set out for the journey home.

Chapter 13

The body was discovered by a jogger early the next morning. The poor man thought at first that someone had been fly tipping on seeing a large mound in the middle of the path but as he got closer, he realised that it was a man. The police arrived and cordoned off the immediate area to preserve the scene for the forensics team. They knew that they would, at some point, end up having to search the whole park and they were not happy about it.

The jogger repeated his story again to the detective who had arrived. How many times had he told the story? How many more times would he have to tell the story? He was trying to keep fit by taking exercise, but this morning's incident had left him wanting a cigarette. That was bad considering that he hadn't smoked for four years.

The scene of crime officers trooped up the path in their white suits followed by the medical examiner who stood shaking his head when he saw the size of the corpse. They were going to need some extra help removing this body. Within the search area, there were leaves, twigs, litter, and the footprint. Every item that could be removed was placed in a little bag and the footprint was photographed several times and then the blood sampled.

An unfortunate forensics officer was chosen to rummage through the victim's pockets in search of identification. A wallet was removed and the corpse was given a name. Edward John Stringer. A detective arrived and would soon find out that Mr Stringer had been released from prison a few months before after serving a sentence for fraud.

The grave but breathless reporter was back and managed to talk for several minutes about a murder where no details of the victim's name or the circumstances of his death had been released. It was not until the evening news bulletin on the Sunday that more information was divulged. As Detective Inspector Nash sat watching the news, his telephone rang and he looked at the screen on his mobile to see the name Adam Ashton.

He answered the call with "Yes I'm watching the news too."

Mike was six-foot-tall with dark brown hair and blue eyes. He had a friendly open smile, which was often used to disarm the people he was about to interrogate. It had been his weekend with his child, and he had fed her burgers and sweets in direct contravention of his wife's orders. Phoebe loved him for it and the ex-hated him for it, job done.

His ex-wife Maria wasn't really a bad person. The hours he worked and the late-night drinks with colleagues had eaten away at Maria's patience and, eventually, he had been asked to move out of the marital home. Mike knew that the breakdown of their marriage was his fault and he had hoped that, after a period of reflection for both of them, they could be reconciled. They may have had a chance were it not for the fact that a new man took his place with, he considered, indecent haste. Since the arrival of Gavin, her new boyfriend, he had taken every opportunity to ruffle Maria's feathers.

Maria was a good-looking woman. She was tall and willowy and had dark hair and dark eyes. From the moment they met, Mike was sure that they would get married. Just over a year later, they were wed and, two years later, Phoebe arrived. Mike progressed through the ranks to Detective Inspector by working long hours and being tenacious in his pursuit of criminals. He formed a habit of spending a lot of time at work and then socialising with his colleagues. Maria was not happy.

The arrival of their daughter had been such a happy time. Somewhere along the line, the job had taken precedence and the arguments started. Maria could see what was happening, but Mike could not. He was missing their daughter's childhood, time that he would never be able to get back.

She found that she was constantly lonely. At times, it was like being a single parent. Maria asked Mike to spend more time at home. She begged him when he ignored her initial pleas and then she shouted at him when that failed too. Getting home of an evening, signalled a start to hostilities where they either argued or stalked around each other in a tense silence.

In the end, Maria had reluctantly decided to ask Mike to leave. Phoebe was older now and was surely hearing the arguments and feeling the tension in the house and she did not want her subjected to it. On request, Mike packed his bags and left and a couple of months later, she was swept off her feet by the handsome charming Gavin.

Mike and Adam briefly discussed the news item. The similarity of the murder to that of Simon Butler was noted and they would put a call in first thing Monday morning to the Detective who was handling it, to trade information. So far, all they knew was that the victim was a fraudster who had just come out of prison and been stabbed. It was enough to provoke their interest and hopefully, if it was the same careful killer, they had left a clue.

On Monday morning, Mike called the Detective who was handling the murder case. Roger Townsend was nearing retirement and was not best pleased that a murder had occurred on his, normally, quiet patch. He and Mike were part of the same territorial force but worked in different locations.

As Roger listened to Mike's description of the murder in his area, the nature of the victim, the single stab wound to the jugular vein, and the lack of evidence he agreed that it could have been done by the same perpetrator. He told Mike about the smudged footprint but admitted that it had no clear discernible features and they could only guess that the foot that made it was about a size nine or ten. The main thing Roger gleaned from their conversation was a way to offload this case onto Mike and get back to planning his retirement.

Some detectives were very territorial, and Mike had worried that Roger Townsend wouldn't want to hand over the case. He was, therefore, very pleased that Roger capitulated at the first suggestion from him. Roger admitted that he was hoping to offload the case. He would probably have to pass the file over soon any way, unless they secured a quick conviction, which seemed unlikely.

Mike went to visit the Chief Inspector to update him on his phone call with Roger and to confirm that it was okay for him to handle both murders. During that conversation, the words "serial killer" were used for the first time. The Chief Inspector had advised caution. If the press and public thought that a serial killer was on the loose, there would be frenzy. Every person ever known to the victims would be tracked down and questioned by the press before they got to them and speculation would abound. They had all seen instances where an innocent person was named by the journalists as a suspect and their lives had been ruined.

The notes and photographs from the first murder were retrieved and a board was set up with two photographs at the top, one of Simon Butler and one of Eddie Stringer. The detectives started on the process of tracing the friends and family of Eddie and were hoping that there was something in their backgrounds which would link the two men. A person known to both of them. A place that they both frequented maybe.

Mike had never worked on a serial killer case before. Suddenly there were far more resources available to him than there had ever been. He had uniformed officers out rounding up Eddie's former associates, scanning through CCTV, canvassing the area, and doing a thorough search of the park. Adam couldn't believe his luck at finding himself assisting on the case. He strutted around the office with an air of importance which was deeply annoying to all the other, more seasoned, detectives.

Both murders had taken place in their area, which was of interest. Being on the edge of a city in the commuter belt meant that the transport links were good and people were very mobile. There was a vast range of clientele available to a con artist based in the area. Could the killer be local or had he travelled from another part of the country because the people he was after were here? It was another question to add to the list of things to investigate.

Everyone on the force seemed to have a reason to be in the office on the day that Eddie's former girlfriend Justine came in to be interviewed. The surgically enhanced self-styled model was no longer in her prime, but everybody wanted to take a peek at someone who most of them had seen featured in magazines. Justine showed little emotion at having to discuss her former boyfriend's demise. In fact, she showed little emotion or interest in anything they discussed. It was as if when the silicon was put in, the personality was taken out.

When Justine left the interview room, she walked through the station smiling and waving like a film star. Maybe she had made some films. If she had, Mike imagined that they would not be PG. The interview had revealed the names of some of Eddie's entourage who, it transpired, had all disappeared when the gravy train dried up. They would all be interviewed as soon as they could be tracked down. Edward John Stringer had been drinking alone in a pub before he met his death on a dark path. Considering the devastation to pensioners, for God's sake, he had left in his wake, it was hard to feel sorry for him.

Chapter 14

When Eve had returned from dispatching Eddie, she had put Dorothea's car in the garage and let herself into the house through the back door. Penny and Dorothea were sat in the kitchen and saw a grinning Eve enter the room.

"Job done, the guest is no more." she exclaimed.

The ladies high fived each other and Dorothea poured them all a glass of sherry. It was a bit late at night to be drinking champagne.

In the morning, they would empty the boot of the car. They didn't want to be rustling about out there at that time of night in case they attracted attention. The scooter was given a thorough cleaning, particularly around the wheels, and was then repackaged. Nobody would know that it had ever been used. The coverall and the wigs and clothes that had been used were put in a box, which Penny stashed in the lock up garage, still in her husband's name. Everything related to the murders found its way there for storage. No one in Penny's family knew about the garage and, if for some reason they were to become suspects, there would be time to get there and dispose of the contents.

The next day as the ladies drank tea, they watched the television news reporter give the scant details available about a body that had been found at six thirty on Saturday morning.

"That was good then. Plenty of time for the strong wind last night to blow all kinds of stuff into and out of the crime scene," Dorothea observed.

Eve told them about the footprint and how she had hopped into the bushes. "They'll be looking for a one-legged man with a size nine foot who can fly," laughed Penny.

Eddie Stringer had been even more revolting in the flesh than he had been in the photographs Eve explained. "You can't get the aroma of booze and sweat from a picture. Believe me, the hot tub plan would have been a very bad idea."

The ladies weren't blasé, but they couldn't see anything that would lead the police to their doors at this time. The disguises were working well, and Eve was adamant that no witnesses had seen her on the path or emerging from her thicket. The footprint indicating that the killer was most likely a man would actually work in their favour.

The ladies wanted the details of the killing. This time Dorothea didn't object to hearing all the more gruesome points as well. Eve explained how someone had walked past her hiding place ten minutes before Eddie arrived.

"I could tell from the footsteps that it wasn't big, fat, wobbly Eddie. When he did come along, the puffing and plodding let me know it was him for sure. I checked that all was clear. I was thinking about all the advice you have me."

"Oh my God, Penny, she listened to us."

"He started to turn around, it was like watching a large battleship trying to execute a turn. He looked completely baffled when he saw me coming towards him and hadn't even raised his arms in defence. I simply reached up and sunk the knife into his neck. The knife had to be pushed in a long way to get through the layers of fat."

This last detail proved a little too much for Dorothea who got up and went to put the kettle on while Eve carried on with her story. Once she had suppressed her urge to faint or be sick, Dorothea returned to the table with a fresh pot of tea and hoped that there would be no more graphic details for her to contend with.

The dinner party guest had crashed to the floor with a stunned look on his face. His eyes were wide open as he breathed his last and then gurgled and wheezed. She didn't have time to hang around in case someone came along, so she had hopped to the bushes, slipped out of her suit, and made her way back to the thicket. She hadn't seen a soul on her way back.

She told her friends about the move with the mobile phone and how she had made good time once off the high street whizzing along on her scooter.

"If anyone looked out of their window, they would have thought I was a teenager, I think.

The streets were deserted though so I don't anticipate any problems."

They arranged to meet at Penny's the next day for their traditional Sunday lunch. Eve wondered which joint of meat Penny was going to incinerate this week. They looked at the papers and drank tea like they usually did. The roast beef which Penny served was crispy on the outside but not too over cooked in the middle and they ate everything that was served to them.

The second murder had been completed and, in a strange way, the ladies were beginning to feel better. Their appetites were certainly alright.

"Well done Penny, that was one of your best Sunday lunches. I really enjoyed that beef. I'm nicely full and I'm feeling rather content too." Eve sat back in her chair and smiled at her friends.

“I agree, about the beef and about the feelings. In fact, I’m grateful enough for the fine dinner to volunteer to do the washing up.” Dorothea collected the plates, giving Eve and Penny a hug as she passed their chairs.

Rather than obsess about the damage that had been done to them, they were now taking action and fighting back. They had been hanging onto their feelings through inertia and now they were exorcising them by doling out their own form of justice.

In the evening, after there had been some afternoon napping, more details of the murder were relayed by the reporter. He looked positively gleeful to be talking about another crime. The victim was confirmed as Edward John Stringer and his despicable crimes against the elderly were brought up. The reporter advised that further details of the case were not being released by the police at that time.

"I wonder if they have linked the two killings," Dorothea said.

"If they have, I would imagine that they would be thoroughly confused at this point," Eve mused.

"Let's hope so," Penny added.

The three friends sat in silent contemplation for some time and eventually Dorothea said what they were all thinking. "We've got away with it so far but I think we should lie low for a while and wait until the police are not so hyper vigilant."

Everyone agreed that this was a good idea unless, of course, someone came to their attention that they could not ignore.

On Monday morning, Eve had arrived at work in the department store and had begun tidying the rails of clothes she could not now afford. Her two colleagues appeared and began discussing the murder of Eddie Stringer. One of them knew someone who knew someone that had been caught out by his scam. They looked at Eve sheepishly as they realised that she had been the victim of a scam too.

"Oh, don't mind me." she said. "You can't spend your whole life on regrets and what ifs. I've moved on." She gave her co-workers a brave smile and then moved away. If only they knew what Eve had done to help her move on.

***

Penny delivered the box of potential evidence to the lock up garage on her way to work at the accountants'.

"I was watching the news about that man that was murdered Eddie Stringer," she told her boss. "How exactly do those boiler room scam things work? Was it like what happened to me and Derek?"

It was a little unkind to embarrass him like that but it established her, pretend, lack of understanding about fraud and reminded him why he employed her.

***

Dorothea's son Malcolm was coming to visit her that evening and she was busy doing housework and checking that nothing related to the crime was in the house. All notes and diagrams had been destroyed by burning after the completion of the operation and everything that they needed to keep was taken away by Penny to the lock up garage. They had all vowed, however, to remain constantly vigilant about ensuring that nothing could link them to the murders. What they said and what they did were just as important as the physical things. She knew that she would have a little smile to herself though when Malcolm asked if she had been up to anything.

All of them at some time during that day had thought about Martin Cole. They were doing their bit to rid the world of fraudsters, but he had conned them. With him, it was personal. They could go on to kill another dozen or so but he would always be there in the background eating away at their souls and rekindling their anger. It would not be long before they had to have a serious talk about whether Martin Cole should be the recipient of one of Eve's lethal visits.

Chapter 15

For the moment, Martin Cole was safe from the ladies as he was still in prison. He was given a five-year sentence which meant that in a few weeks he would have served his two and a half years and would be released. He saw the news of the murders of two fraudsters. It barely registered with him as he did not consider his self to be a fraudster. He was just an investment manager whose luck had run out.

Martin Cole was the king of denial. He hadn't conned people out of money, and he wasn't a gambling addict. A counsellor visited him when he arrived in prison to discuss his addiction, but Martin had been resistant to his attempts. He was in prison and was not able to place any bets and he hadn't gone cold turkey, so he obviously didn't have a problem. He was asked how often he went to the bookmakers and how much money he thought he had gone through. The counsellor wanted to know why he had used his clients' money to place bets if he wasn't an addict. He explained that he used it because it was there.

He had no remorse. When he got out of prison, he would have to take some low paid job and keep his head down. Once he was no longer being monitored by the probation service, he would find a less onerous way of earning a living. He expected a certain standard of living and would attain it in any way he could.

Before he had been caught, Martin Cole was living the type of life he knew he deserved. He bought a sports car and expensive suits and jewellery. His mother told him from early childhood through to her death five years before, how special he was. She had schooled him in good manners and etiquette so that he could mix with nice people. His father had turned up occasionally, usually when he needed money or a place to stay. His mother always tried to accommodate him and never said anything bad about him. She was perfect.

His mother worked two jobs and wore threadbare clothes because all her money was spent on Martin. He developed a taste for the good things in life. His manners and politeness made him popular. Martin found that being charming and persuasive came easily to him. The only thing that didn't ever develop properly was his conscience.

His good education had made it easy for him to find employment in the finance industry. He was attracted to the life of a city trader. He would, of course, be successful and then he could buy a sports car and a smart apartment and look after his mother. The truth was that Martin was never any good at his chosen profession. He liked the high risk aspect of trading but didn't know when to call it quits. He was special so he thought that the normal rules didn't apply to him.

Martin managed to talk his way into two further jobs in the city after he was asked to leave his first one. His reputation as a liability eventually spread and he was not able to talk himself into a fourth job. He had been gambling with other people's money and he missed the adrenaline rush that came with it. It was almost inevitable that he would start gambling with his own money.

When his beloved mother had been diagnosed with cancer, he was quite upset. He was more upset three months later when she was no longer able to cook and do housework. She was taken to the hospital weekly for her chemotherapy and had a huge pile of drugs which she had to take each day. The prognosis was not good but the doctor hoped that, with the proper care, she would live for a couple of years. Martin watched his mother get weaker and weaker and be of less and less use around the house. His decision to expedite her passing was not an act of kindness; it was more about relieving his burden.

For the last couple of weeks of her life, Martin dutifully passed her aspirin, paracetamol, or ibuprofen rather than the drugs which she had been prescribed. She didn't know what she was taking but looked lovingly at her son who was caring for her. He hadn't actually killed her, he reasoned, but he had certainly not helped. The doctor advised him that she had succumbed more quickly than he had anticipated. Some people just gave up, he said.

Unencumbered by the one moral person in his life, Martin had decided to get the life he wanted in any way he could. The council house where they lived was in his mother's name and he needed somewhere to live, somewhere nice to live. He set out to research ways to make money on the internet and stumbled across details of the less legitimate schemes that people had used. He put a lot of work into organising the Ponzi scheme that he was setting up. Paperwork and brochures were produced for the dummy investment company. He had spent a lot of time designing the logo. It had to say steady reliability. He had settled on a shield featuring a crown and a lion. Protection, Britishness, and a hint of aristocracy would appeal to the moneyed middle classes on whom he would prey.

He had never been keen on the hard sell technique. He would meet his, would be, investors and chat to them like an old friend and then describe the many, imagined, successes of his career in the city. He complimented the women and looked at photos of the grandchildren. All of his clients liked him and happily recommended him to their friends. Having done a lot of ground work on investments for the brochure, Martin thought, at one stage, that he might actually try to make the money work. Well, he might put some of the funds into the investments. In the end, he didn't put any in, he spent it all on gambling.

At the end, Martin realised that his plot was unravelling. He had chased one bad bet with another and another and finally risked a large bet hoping to recoup his losses. The rent was due on his luxury apartment and the dividend payments were due to go out as well. When the horse didn't romp home, he made a quick exit via Gatwick to Marbella. He hoped to get a job selling time shares. He would be brilliant at that. His glittering career in sales was cut short when he had been arrested.

Chapter 16

Adam and Mike were staring at the board in the office hoping that some miraculous revelation would appear to them. The report from the forensic team, when condensed, revealed that they had found a footprint. Every other test had drawn a blank. The search of the park had revealed no murder weapon and nothing that could confidently be claimed to relate to the murder. There was a trampled area within a thick tangle of bushes which had aroused their interest, but it could be an area where children had made a camp. The soil in the park had been walked over so many times that nothing was distinct. The mass of leaves on the floor within the thicket meant that there were no footprints there at all.

The CCTV pictures had shown a man exiting the path but after an appeal, he had come forward and been eliminated from the enquiry.

Another camera showed a teenager, they couldn't tell if it was a boy or a girl, leaving the park on a scooter. The scooter rider stopped to look at their phone, taking their time to do so. Not the actions of someone who may have witnessed a murder or seen someone who was likely covered in blood. The police asked via the media for anybody who was in the area to come forward, but the teenager never materialised.

Every person who they had listed had been interviewed and all the victims' known associates had been investigated and their backgrounds checked. They could find no one who was linked to both murders.

"The only piece of physical evidence we have is a bloody footprint which is indistinct around the edges." Mike turned to Adam waiting for him to make a contribution.

"Just one footprint. That's really weird." Was all he could say.

Shortly, Mike would be going to see the chief inspector to update him on the murder cases and he had nothing to report which gave them any indication as to who was responsible. As he was about to leave his desk, he glanced at the morning's newspaper and noticed an article about a citizens' arrest on a graffiti artist. The person who had carried out the arrest was well known in the area for making regular patrols and had been referred to as a vigilante. Maybe that was what they were looking at with these cases, a vigilante killer.

"Good morning Sir." Mike was waved into a seat and the Chief looked at him expectantly.

He filled the next five minutes with the results of the last interviews, confirmed that the forensic team had not found anything, and finished by mentioning the footprint. His boss did not look pleased.

"I think we might be dealing with a vigilante," he said. "in which case the suspect pool has just increased to every man who wears a size nine or ten shoe."

Once he was safely back in the office, Mike thought more about his last minute suggestion that it was a vigilante. If it was, the question that leapt to mind was how was he choosing his victims? He voiced his thoughts to Adam who immediately went onto the internet and found that both their victims had been mentioned in articles in the press a few months before their murders. This information wouldn't help them identify their killer, but it did give an indication as to how the victims were being chosen. They would look at a way to make that information work for them.

He would be having Phoebe at the weekend giving him an opportunity to put his work to the back of his mind, meaning that he might be able to sleep at night. Mike's 5-year-old daughter was collected from her mother's home on Friday evening. As he drew up to what was his former house, he saw Phoebe's face at the window. She was waiting for him to arrive. He had a brief conversation with Maria, in which she reiterated that he wasn't to give their daughter sweets. He nodded in the right places as Phoebe hopped from foot to foot, eager to start her latest adventure with her daddy.

Mike didn't want to be the type of weekend father who took his child to the zoo and then the burger restaurant every time they visited. He planned different activities, some of them educational, and made sure he didn't say anything bad about Maria or Gavin. On Saturday afternoon, they were making cakes, and a mess, which was enjoyable for both of them.

Phoebe gave a big sigh and said, “I’m glad I’m with you. Mummy and Gavin are always shouting.”

Mike was horrified. “Are they shouting at you?”

“Oh no.” Phoebe replied. “At each other.”

It was with some difficulty that Mike suppressed his smile. Trouble in paradise. The arrival of Gavin had scuppered that dream. He had Phoebe as his little spy in the camp and he would monitor the situation over the coming weeks. If he could step in and protect Maria from the hateful Gavin or comfort her after he had been kicked out, who knows, he might stand a chance after all.

He had enjoyed his weekend with his daughter but now Detective Inspector Mike Nash was back at work and focused on the job in hand. A list of fraudsters currently living in the commuter belt area was obtained. Both murders had been near to the city, so they assumed there was a reason for this. Adam was searching the internet for any fraudster who had been featured in the media in the last six months. If they found someone, they would contact them, inform them of the risk of attack, and set up surveillance. They were hoping to observe whoever was watching the potential victim and stop him before he could murder again.

On Thursday morning, Mike read an article in a national paper about the murders which mentioned that stories about both victims had been related in magazines a few months before their demise.

Mike went into the Chief Inspector's office waving the newspaper. "Have you seen this? We finally get a lead and the next thing you know, it's in the papers. If this killer is as smart as I think he is, he's going to change tactics and we have lost an opportunity to catch him. I hope this wasn't the result of a leak from this office."

The chief tried to placate him. "It was an outside chance that we would know who he was going to target next and catch him that way but, yes, it is deeply annoying. I will instigate an investigation to see where the story came from."

The simple truth was that the journalist had done his research and come to the same conclusion as the detectives. When he searched on the internet, he found what Adam had found. Stories had appeared in women's magazines about the two victims by way of warning the readership about the perils faced, firstly of internet dating, and secondly of investing in shares when they were being sold over the phone. The police contacted him and asked how he had got the information and he had said through research. He was adamant that no one from the force had given him a tipoff.

Adam was sat at his desk a little bemused by the sight of Mike practically running through the office with a thunderous look on his face heading towards the Chief Inspector's room. When he was shown the article in the newspaper, he understood why he was so mad.

"Do we carry on with the plan?" Adam enquired.

"We'll have to" Mike said, "it's all we've got."

Chapter 17

Dorothea saw the article in the paper and phoned the others to let them know. They would meet as usual on Sunday and discuss how this would affect any future plans.

"We think we're so clever but we didn't think of this problem. We could have walked straight into a trap." Eve was pacing up and down as she spoke to Dorothea and Penny. "Thank God that particular piece of information found its way into the papers."

Penny had been thinking and waved her hand as if asking permission to speak. "Let's think of this as an opportunity. If we now find a new guest in a different way, it will throw them even further off the scent. You've been to the lock up and seen all those old magazines that Derek kept. There has to be something in one of them."

They agreed to make a trip to the lock up the following Wednesday, when neither Penny nor Eve were working, to see what they could find.

The three ladies sat inside the lock up garage surrounded by boxes. They had found the more recent magazines and papers, from about three years before, and were searching through them for a new dinner party guest. Dorothea brought some sandwiches and coffee and Penny brought some cakes. As they read article after article, the conversation turned to their nemesis Martin Cole.

"At some point," said Eve, "he is going to have to pay. I don't think this will be over for any of us until he is dead."

The garage was stacked full of boxes and bags. There was old furniture and obsolete electrical equipment. The ladies were using a large box as a makeshift table for their picnic.

"What did you think when you first came in here and saw all this?" asked Dorothea.

Penny considered the question and then replied with brutal honesty. "I was furious. I was still angry with him for killing himself and then I found that he had never conquered his hoarding problem, he had just moved it somewhere else. Don't forget that I discovered it two years ago and I've visited it many times since then. Each time I've come here, I've thrown stuff away so you can imagine what it was like the first time I opened the door."

Eve looked around her at the piles that were still there. "Did you find any treasure?" she asked.

"Only a gun. I didn't think I'd ever have a use for that. I'll get through it all eventually but I don't hold out much hope of finding anything of value."

The ladies each had a pile of magazines next to them and they were flicking through each one looking for a story on a suitable fraudster. Eve and Penny were flicking through, Dorothea kept finding articles which were interesting and becoming absorbed in them. Her pile was about twice the size of the other two because she was taking much longer. The search was suspended when Penny began flourishing a magazine above her head.

"Oh, I've got one." Penny was waving excitedly.

A burly builder called John Hall had carried out repairs to the roofs of the elderly and then charged them thousands of pounds instead of the few hundred it should have cost. Once he had ensnared an elderly customer, he returned again and again in the guise of a caring friend, found more jobs to do, and grossly overcharged for them. When he was confronted on one occasion by a concerned relative, he threatened violence. Someone had called his bluff and reported him to the police, and he had been arrested and subsequently convicted. The paper reported that he had previous convictions for similar offences.

Dorothea studied the picture that accompanied the article which showed a bull necked, tattooed man. He was described as six-foot-tall and weighing eighteen stone. When he asked for money, people weren't going to ask questions, they just paid.

"This one looks as if he would fight back. Yes, he is a thoroughly evil man, but we cannot risk taking him on."

Eve was quick to reply, "We can't dismiss it straight away just because it's problematic. This is the type of man that won't stop until he's dead. I propose we do some research and see what we can come up with and only give up if it seems impossible."

The wigs and the tablet computer were retrieved from their box and a new operation was set in motion. Penny was sent off to a different cafe with wi-fi, to see what she could find out about John Hall. There were many articles relating to his life of crime and pictures of his younger brothers who had become embroiled in a number of his schemes. He had been married but his wife left him after years of domestic violence and took his daughters. A bleak report in a local newspaper told how he terrorised his wife. Much of his anger had been fuelled by alcohol as he berated his wife for having given birth to daughters and not a longed for son.

The three ladies listened to Penny's report and resolved to find a way to deal with this pig of a man. He was a drinker, as they were almost certain he would be, and if he drank himself into a stupor that could work to their advantage again. The tools of their trade, the wigs, the tape for the number plates and their charity shop clothes were shared out and the serious business began. John Hall lived further away than their previous victims but there was no obstacle that they couldn't overcome when it came to dealing with this thug.

The operation to neutralise the latest guest was proving frustrating. John Hall was a more mercurial man than their previous two victims. Simon Butler had seldom left his house, or his chair, and Eddie Stringer kept to a routine. John sometimes went out to work and sometimes he didn't, he drank in a number of different pubs, with no discernible pattern to his visits, and he had been seen bringing women back to his shabby house. Dorothea, Penny, and Eve could not even begin to imagine what these women saw in someone like John Hall.

After a month of covert surveillance, the ladies were no nearer to finding a suitable time or place to carry out the deed. They had however seen him cruising around areas where bungalows were prevalent in his van. He seemed to be looking for his next elderly victim. Penny said that maybe this would have to be a two-person job. She would be happy to wave the gun around and Eve could slip in and use the knife.

They were learning the art of patience, Dorothea said. One could not go up against someone like John without a solid plan. Something would happen and they would get their chance. All of them felt that their missions were important and that some act of fate would intervene to give them an opportunity. They just wished that whatever it was would hurry up and reveal itself.

Chapter 18

Mike and Adam decided, despite the newspaper article, they would proceed with their plan of searching for potential victims mentioned in the media. They had no other leads or forensic evidence except for the indistinct footprint so although it wasn't likely to produce a result, it was all they could do. They would have to hope that the killer hadn't picked up on the piece in the newspaper and would stick to his modus operandi.

The detectives had been making a list of people with convictions for fraud and then searching to see if they had been mentioned recently in magazines. The list of offences committed by the fraudsters made for bleak reading. There were so many ways that people could perpetrate a fraud. Men and women in positions of trust within a company or an organisation could help themselves to funds.

There were Ponzi schemes and boiler room operations. Some family members stole money from elderly relatives. A great many rogue builders were unearthed and then there was the internet.

As Mike read about the number of people that paid for goods that had never been delivered, he felt like he was losing his faith in mankind. A common scam was carried out on those selling too. An overpayment was made for the goods and the seller was asked to hand over the goods and cash because they had received too much. After the goods and cash were passed over, the payment would be cancelled by the buyer, leaving the seller without the item they were selling and a sum of money. Phishing, as it was called, was another con. It was a way of getting people to reveal their bank details and PINs by sending emails purporting to be from a bank.

Adam shook his head as he read another report. "I'm reading about a gang who called at pensioners' houses and pretended to be police officers. They say that the person has been the subject of a fraud and ask for their credit and debit cards because they are needed as evidence. I can see why someone might want to murder these crooks."

They were both extremely dispirited and headed for the local pub after work to try to numb the pain.

A lot of the frauds they looked into could be eliminated because they did not involve the right sort of criminal. They doubted that their killer would be interested in someone who had ripped off a company and many of the internet and credit card cons involved large gangs of people. It was often unclear who the head man was. Simon Butler and Eddie Stringer had targeted vulnerable women and pensioners respectively. Their vigilante was meting out justice on behalf of the weak and downtrodden.

At the end of four weeks' work, Mike and Adam had three names in front of them. Two of them were tenuous leads at best. They involved people who stole from the companies they worked for. They decided to focus on their third fraudster, Dean Robertson, a builder who overcharged his elderly customers, and left a catalogue of shoddy work behind him. They spoke to Dean on the phone and arranged for him to come into the station. It had taken a lot of assurances to persuade him to attend an interview. They finally pointed out that they could just come and drag him out of his home in front of his wife and children and he reluctantly agreed.

Dean Robertson, it transpired, was the classic bully. He was unfazed at taking money from defenceless customers and badgering those who tried to object but now that his life was being threatened, he went to pieces. What were the police going to do? He was demanding around the clock protection by armed officers.

"Dean, we're not saying someone is after you, just that it may be a possibility." Mike explained about the two victims and how they appeared to have been selected.

A court report in a local paper a couple months ago detailed Dean's failure to pay a fine and mentioned his previous convictions. This small item had probably gone under the perpetrator's radar but they had to bring the risk to his attention.

***

In the beginning, Dean did not set out to be a conman. He was simply a bad builder, a bad lazy builder. He cut corners and used inferior materials and sometimes didn't finish jobs at all. He found that preying on the elderly was the answer to his problems. The pensioners for whom he did work did not know how much a job should cost or how long it should take. They were also less likely to complain.

He had two children with his present girlfriend and a child from a previous relationship. Dean had no choice, he told himself, but to make money any way he could so that he could support his kids. He didn't take into account the fact that he rarely bothered to pay for his first child and was frequently dragged to court when the arrears built up. He didn't take into account the amount of money he spent in the pub or at the bookies either.

As Dean panicked and seemed close to tears, Mike fervently wished that they had left him to his fate. Mike tried to explain to the quivering Dean that they would be watching his house in a covert way hoping to discover someone doing the same thing. The killer was very organised and would not make a move without making his own observations. Dean left the police station and headed straight to the nearest DIY store. Within hours, he had fitted security lights to the front and back of his house and he then went online to order some CCTV cameras. This was not what Mike had wanted, but he couldn't really blame him for putting those safeguards in place.

For the next three weeks, Dean Robertson called the police at least once a night.

"Hello, I need help."

"Is that Dean Robertson?"

"Yes, how did you know?"

"I recognised your voice. What can we do for you tonight?"

"The security lights in the back garden have gone off again."

"I believe that Detective Nash has spoken to you about this. It's probably an animal, a cat or a fox. Can you hear anyone in your garden?"

"No."

"If you actually hear someone trying to get into your house, call us. Otherwise, Dean, stay off the phone."

In addition to the lights and cameras, Dean bought a big dog.

Over the following weeks, nothing even vaguely suspicious occurred so the operation was scaled back. Dean added extra locks to his doors and spent his time either secured in his fortress or accompanied by a couple of large friends should he have to go outside. Adam commented that instilling a sense of paranoia in the loathsome Dean almost made the whole thing worth it.

Once again, Detective Inspector Mike Nash was sitting in a chair in the Chief Inspector's office giving him bad news. All they could do now was continue searching the media for likely victims or wait for their killer to make a mistake. It wasn't much but it was all they could do. Another detective would be brought in to review the information that had been gathered so far. A fresh pair of eyes, the Chief had said. Mike didn't argue with what could be seen as a lack of confidence in his work. He would take any help he could get.

He lived for the weekends that he spent with Phoebe. It was like pushing a reset button that enabled him to shrug off the fatigue and hopelessness that dogged his life towards the end of every fortnight. He wanted to have fun with his child and had therefore been wary of bringing up the subject of Maria and Gavin fighting. He didn't want to worry his daughter and he didn't want her to report back to his ex-wife either. He would wait until the time was right rather than force the issue. For now, he was feeding her a taboo ice lolly and relishing the joy on her face.

Chapter 19

Dorothea phoned Penny and Eve and arranged an emergency meeting. The ladies arrived eager to find out what was going on. The news was not about a breakthrough in the problem of John Hall as·they had hoped. Dorothea had heard from her eldest son Robert who was going to be visiting from America. He would be arriving in two weeks' time, accompanied by his wife Melanie and their son and daughter, and would be staying with his mother.

"We'll have to put everything on hold until after he's left."

Eve sank into a chair and sighed.

"Are you disappointed?" asked Dorothea.

"Yes and no," Eve replied. "I think we would all like to get rid of the guest, but we could do with a break."

Penny agreed. "I have been neglecting my girls and grandchildren. Let's take the summer off and get back to work after the school holidays. It's too light of an evening now to undertake a night attack and people are more likely to be out late when the weather is good."

As the tea was being made, Penny studied her friend Eve. Dorothea had her boys and she had her family, but Eve had no one. They would fill their summers with outings with their grandchildren; what would Eve do? They would do some Sunday lunches, of course, but not every week. Penny explained her concerns to Dorothea on the phone later. They would both have to ensure that they included Eve in some of their family trips without making it seem like charity.

Robert lived in America where he coached football, or soccer as the Americans called it, at a university. He led a charmed life, settling abroad with his wife and two children doing a job he loved. He agonised about whether to return to England when his father died but his mother had been adamant that he stayed where he was. It would have been a wrench to leave such a good life behind and he was grateful to his mother for making the decision easier for him.

Dorothea's sons talked about their father's death each time they spoke on the phone or over the internet. Mostly they discussed how their mother was coping and what they would like to do to that Martin Cole if they got hold of him. Robert had been tormented by his decision to stay in America but as the months passed, Malcolm reported that Dorothea was doing better with the help of her two new friends.

He could see the change in his mother when he saw her on the computer screen. She talked about things other than anger and loss although he was sure they were still there beneath the surface. She spent some time every week with her friends Penny and Eve and they supported each other through their troubles. He had, of course, come home for his father's funeral and he had returned again at the end of the trial to see Martin Cole sent to prison.

He was surprised at his mother's rejection of the church. Although Robert and Malcolm had lapsed soon after they left home, the church had always been an integral part of his parents' lives. Who would still believe in a God when they had lost their life savings and their husband, he supposed. He worried that she would be lost without the guidance of her faith, but she now had Penny and Eve.

During their visit, Robert wanted to spend as much time with his mother as possible so that she could see her grandchildren Rick and Tamara. If he was living in the UK, he would have called on her all the time, so they had to pack a year's worth of visits to granny into three weeks.

Dorothea's house had been stripped of anything relating to the murders and their gear had been put back into storage. She felt a lightness as she anticipated her family's arrival but also a sense of unease because of their unfinished business.

Penny and Dorothea had agreed to include Eve in their plans. The end of her son's visit would be marked by a big party with her other son Malcolm, Penny, her daughters and their families, and Eve. She would have a lot of cooking to do which she loved.

Joy and laughter tumbled into the house with her grandchildren. Tears of happiness flowed and granny fed everyone. The children had made a list of places that they wanted to visit, which they showed Dorothea, their voices getting higher and more frantic as each place was discussed. Robert and Melanie made the decision to send them to the garden where they could let off steam while the grownups talked.

"So, you really are doing ok?" Robert asked again.

"Of course, I still miss your dad, but I am getting on with my life. My friends Penny and Eve have been so wonderful. Together, we can cope with just about anything. You'll see them while you're here as we're always in and out of each other's houses."

Robert would make sure to thank these ladies when he saw them for all they had done for his mother.

Eve found that she was having a busy summer. She went to museums with Dorothea and her family and to the lido with Penny and her crowd. Every week there was another invitation and she enjoyed being with her friends' grandchildren. Whenever she was invited to eat out with her friends, she tried to pay her way but the families wouldn't let her open her purse. She was aware that the ladies made an effort to include her in their plans and was, as ever, moved by their concern and care. She and everyone else was looking forward to the party that Dorothea was throwing before her son Robert returned to the states.

In the kitchen, Dorothea and her daughter in law Melanie were preparing for the party. She was passing on the recipes that had been cooked by her mother and grandmother back in Trinidad. It was good to spend this time with her daughter in law. The women had been happy to shut themselves in the kitchen, away from the bedlam, where they could chat and become even closer. They were making salt fish balls, tostones, mutton stew, and of course jerk chicken. There were also beef burgers and sausages to cook on the barbecue for the less adventurous as well as a range of salads. She hadn't been sure what Penny's daughters' families would eat but they tried everything and asked for a couple of recipes.

As she looked around the garden at her friends and family chatting and laughing and eating, Dorothea was very happy. She couldn't keep the thought that Royston would have loved this from her mind, but it was a fleeting moment and she went back to enjoying the scene as she watched her and Penny's grandchildren running around. Malcolm organised a game of cricket for the kids who loved the running up and down but weren't at all interested in the rules.

Penny and Eve joined Dorothea on the patio from where they surveyed the activity like queens on their thrones.

Robert, on seeing them all together, took the opportunity to deliver the speech he had been rehearsing. "Eve, Penny, I am so glad that you are here today. This party is for family and friends and, as far as I'm concerned, you fit both categories. You have all supported each other and I know how much your friendship has meant to mum and I want to take this chance to thank you."

All three ladies reached for tissues as the tears welled up in their eyes. No words were necessary; they simply stood up and pulled Robert into a group hug.

"You are all so brave to face what you have gone through and come out the other side as normal people," Robert said.

Eve couldn't help adding, "Nearly normal."

Maybe it was the rum punch that allowed the taboo name to be said. The children were finally exhausted and were sat down with books and Robert began to talk about Martin Cole.

"Is he out of prison yet?" he enquired.

The ladies said that they didn't know, but they were well aware that his release date had passed. Malcolm confirmed that he was. "I've got some friends in the right places who let me know that he was out and where he has gone to live."

This piqued the women's interest, but they had to remain cool.

"Let me know where he is, and I'll be happy to pay him a visit." Robert said as he puffed up his chest. Kirsty and Laura's husbands showed an interest in exacting revenge too.

Dorothea calmed them all down with some wise words. "What would be the point of getting into trouble yourselves over that man. And what if you were caught? No, I've had enough problems due to him."

"Yes," said Penny. "We were the victims and we have put it behind us and you should as well."

"I wish we knew who the Vigilante Killer was and then we could pass his name to him," said Laura.

"The Vigilante Killer?" Penny asked.

"It was in the paper. That is what they are calling the man who killed the two conmen."

Eve, Dorothea and Penny exchanged a furtive look. The "man" who had murdered Simon and Eddie was becoming a major story.

"Vigilante Killer." Said Eve. She quite liked the sound of it.

Chapter 20

How many more times could they go back over the evidence, Mike asked himself? The review by another detective produced nothing new and it had now been five months since the last killing had taken place. The second murder came three months after the first. Had the Vigilante Killer, as he had been dubbed by the press, finished his activity?

A tabloid newspaper editor had decided to feature the murders. Both victims had been stabbed in the neck. Both victims were known fraudsters. A reference to vigilantes had been seized on and the nickname invented. The police and the public had adopted the name and the idea of an avenging murderer, despite their being no confirmation that it was true.

Crime never stopped and they could not keep devoting time and resources to the case. The board with the photographs and lists and timelines was now being used as a coat stand. Adam lost his swagger. It was only good being involved in a serial killer case if you could solve it. As had happened before, other crimes and investigations took priority. The weekly meetings with the Chief Inspector regarding the killings had stopped as they all knew that they had reached an impasse.

At the weekend, Mike would have Phoebe and he could relax and enjoy his daughter and put this failure behind him. This week he was taking her to see his parents. It was an hour's drive away which meant a never-ending game of I Spy, but it was worth it. There had been no mention of the shouting again, but Mike hoped to recruit his parents to the cause and see if they could elicit anything from Phoebe with some gentle questioning.

His mother and Phoebe were sat at the kitchen table drawing as Mike and his father hovered in the hallway just out of sight.

"Will you put the pictures on the fridge?" Phoebe asked.

"Yes, of course. Why don't you do another picture and take it home to mummy for her fridge?" Phoebe looked at her Nana and thought about the question.

"Maybe."

"Only maybe, she would love a picture," Nana prompted and Phoebe shrugged.

The drawing continued for a couple of minutes and then she tried again. "Why don't you want to do a drawing for your mummy?"

Phoebe was full of concentration again as she thought carefully about her answer. "She probably won’t notice 'cause she’s always arguing with Gavin.”

Nana took the opening. “Oh dear, what do they argue about?”

“Money” replied Phoebe.

Assurances came from Nana and Grandpa that they were sure that the arguing would stop soon and the subject was changed to which ice cream flavour would she like, the perfect distraction. Mike’s parents were concerned with what they had heard but more worried about what Mike would do next. They didn’t want him storming around to Maria’s and causing a scene. If Maria stopped him, seeing Phoebe, they wouldn’t be able to see her either. Mike was troubled by the discovery but was at a loss as to what to do. Maria would not take kindly to him interfering in her relationship but he was concerned about the negative effect it was having on Phoebe. He calmed his parents by saying he would give it some thought and not go in all guns blazing.

The reset button hadn't worked so well this weekend because now he was worried about his daughter. When he sat at his desk on Monday morning, he was thinking about Maria and Gavin. On a whim, he searched the police database for any mention of Gavin Vincent. He found something. Gavin did not have a criminal record but he had been the subject of an investigation about a year before he had met Maria. A further search revealed that Gavin had been accused of conning money out of a woman he was dating.

Mike's head was swimming as he read the report which had echoes of Simon Butler. It seemed that Gavin was a much more slippery customer than Simon had been. He played the long game and the money was handed over in small amounts rather than him making outrageous demands for large sums. When he was interviewed, Gavin had been plausible and reasonable saying that the funds he received were for items and expenditure which benefited both him and his, by then former, partner. The woman involved veered between loving him and hating him and eventually the case was dropped.

Mike just wanted to charge around to Maria's and tell her what he found. He took a walk outside the building and gave himself a chance to think it through. He had no cause to search the database for Gavin and that could be a problem. The result could explain why he had been interested. Also, he knew that Maria had, apart from the maintenance he paid her, very little money of her own. There was no secret stash of savings to be pilfered and would he try to con the ex-wife of a detective? The fact that they were arguing about money made Mike hopeful that Gavin had realised that there was no easy money to be prised from Maria and that he would move on soon.

The next time he had his daughter for the weekend, Mike decided to mention the arguments. He would admit that he overheard her talking with Nana and ask if things were better at home. When he broached the subject with Phoebe, she gave a somewhat startling reply.

“They are all happy again. Gavin has a new job where he works at night and they have more money now.”

This information made Mike even more suspicious of Gavin.

***

A couple of nasty home invasion burglaries had happened since Eddie’s murder, where the occupants were threatened with knives and forced to hand over cash, jewellery, phones, and car keys. Mike and Adam were sent to the home of the latest victims to take statements and liaise with the scene of crime officers. He was determined to catch the perpetrators and was glad to have this case rather than turning the nagging doubt about Gavin over and over in his mind. Not to mention two unsolved murders.

These criminals were sloppy. There were footprints outside the house and the stolen car was found partially burnt out on waste ground. The forensics team identified a number of DNA sequences and, once the victims' samples had been eliminated, they found a winner.

The arrest of the robber and his accomplice followed a car chase through country lanes resulting resulted in the offenders crashing and suffering minor injuries. The police were delighted with their day's work. Not only had they caught those responsible, they sped through the country with their sirens wailing which was always an adrenalin rush. Mike, Adam, and practically everyone else at the station decamped to the pub to celebrate a much needed success. They had the DNA evidence, but they also found some of the stolen possessions in the car. If only the Vigilante Killer would make a similar mistake, they would have him.

As he drank his pint, Mike reflected on all the times when he had been drinking when he should have been at home with his wife and daughter. The crowd was getting rowdy as the drinks were consumed, but Mike did not feel in a party mood. The Vigilante Killer murders were unsolved and he was feeling anxious about Gavin.

Chapter 21

Although he made friends easily, Martin Cole never kept them. They were superficial relationships in which he took what he needed from the person, racing tips, knowledge, or money, and then moved on. There was no one to meet him when he left the open prison following his release. He had no home, the house he had shared with his mother was reclaimed by the council and his luxury flat was long gone so the housing development adviser helped him apply to the council for accommodation. He would, initially, be in a hostel.

His time in prison had not been easy. Martin had no interest in making friends with his fellow inmates. They were strangely astute at divining who was an odd ball and they steered clear of Martin, which was fine by him. Serving time for him was a bore. He was an educated man so he didn't want to take any of the courses on offer. There were no books that interested him in the pathetically small library so he watched television and moped.

The thought of living in a single room and sharing the other facilities made Martin very angry. He should have something much better than this. To add to his problems, he was also on probation so he would have to report regularly to his officer and be questioned and badgered about finding gainful employment. With a criminal record, he was not going to find the type of job he wanted, one which gave access to money so he would have to take some low paid job until an opportunity to make some real cash came along.

The people that ran the hostel sat him down and said they would help him apply for benefits. The kindly lady asked him if he needed help filling out the forms. Martin had been ecstatic on being freed but now he was entering a new kind of hell. He informed the well meaning woman that he had received a first class education and was quite capable of completing the forms. His tact and charm temporarily deserted him.

The room that Martin was given was very small. The single bed was no better than the one at the prison. If he wanted to use the bathroom, he had to go to one down the hall. There was a small kitchen next to a recreational area which had some uncomfortable looking chairs and a tiny television. The set in the prison was much bigger than this one. He almost felt like asking to go back.

The only good thing about the hostel was that it gave him the motivation to find a job quickly and get out of the place. He scanned the wanted section of the local paper for something suitable. He had great confidence that, once in front of a potential employer, he could talk himself into work. He knew he would have to aim quite low but he was adamant when he spoke to the probation officer that he wouldn't be labouring on a building site. His mother would have been horrified to see him become a navvy, as she called them.

In the end, Martin was forced to take a job at a factory on a production line. It was beneath him, of course, but it would give him the money that he desperately needed to find a new place to live. The boss of the company, Mr Evans, where they turned chicken into burgers and nuggets and other bread crumbed products, proudly showed Martin the production process. Slabs of processed chicken were fed into machines and cut to size before travelling onwards to be covered in some gloop, he was told what it was, but he had stopped listening by then. The burgers, nuggets, or whatever continued their journey through quality control to packing.

Mr. Evans advised Martin that he would be in the warehouse where the individual packs were put into large boxes and then onto vans. The endless spiel continued as Mr. Evans recited the names of the many, many chains of shops which bought his products. The only merciful thing about being in the warehouse was that he would be wearing overalls not the hairnet and white coat that they wore on the actual line. Martin could have wept as he listened to his new boss tell him about the career progression opportunities available to him if he worked hard.

On his first day at his new job, Martin was assigned a locker and given a pair of overalls; he would have to wash them himself, he was told, and was sent to the warehouse manager. It was like being in prison again but he would have to work harder. The other workers weren't unfriendly but they weren't friendly either. That suited him as he did not intend to stick around long enough to worry about teamwork and career progression. Martin did an acceptable amount of work, no more or no less, and, at the end of the day, he returned to his hostel exhausted. Manual work, he decided, was not for him.

The only manual work Martin had ever done involved picking up his sun lounger and moving it to a better position when he lived, all too briefly, in Spain. There was a particular way of stacking the boxes which had been explained to him several times by his co-worker. They treated him as if he were a moron. He was Martin Cole and he did not like it.

As much as he already hated it, the next day Martin reported for duty at the allotted time and punched his card. He put on his overall and walked slowly to find the warehouse manager and find out what delight awaited him. He was informed that he would be packing the boxes today with Jimmy, who would show him how it was done. Someone was going to show him how to put one box into another box, brilliant. Martin felt wretched as he was led across the room to this latest incarnation of hell. He had already developed an aversion to all chicken and breadcrumb products.

Jimmy met him in the packing area and led him over to the large boxes.

“Grab one of those,” he instructed.

Martin noted Jimmy’s shuffling walk and his slow speech and realised that he was handicapped in some way. Good God, could this get any worse. As he picked up a box as instructed, he was rewarded with a beaming smile from Jimmy who then proceeded to tell him how to put boxes into boxes.

His colleague was about thirty years old. He had a childlike quality which made it difficult to determine his age exactly. His light brown hair was slightly too long and his overall was slightly too big, which contributed to his youthful appearance. Martin wondered about Jimmy's age but it was just a fleeting thought. He didn't care about Jimmy or how old he was. This man had nothing to offer him, he decided. Martin would soon learn something that changed his mind.

There was no bullying or baiting of Jimmy by his fellow workers. They were patient with him and protective of him. When he gave out the big Jimmy smile, you couldn't help but smile back. The morning passed relatively quickly and, at lunchtime, Martin sat with Jimmy in the small canteen and listened to his story.

Chapter 22

Before his accident, Jimmy said, he had been normal. He was a passenger in a car that was side swiped and he had been very badly injured. As he was thrown around in the car, he hit his head and was knocked unconscious. He remained unconscious for three weeks and when he awoke, his life had changed. Well, he was told it had changed. He remembered bits and pieces from before the accident, his family, and playing as a child but he did not remember being normal. He only knew he was different because people told him.

His leg was badly broken and had to be pinned and he had also broken his pelvis. It took months to learn to walk and speak again because of the brain damage he had suffered as well as the physical injuries. Martin listened seemingly sympathetically to Jimmy's story and was beginning to get bored when he mentioned something very interesting. The accident was someone else's fault and he had received a large amount of compensation from an insurance company. Martin went straight into conman mode and asked Jimmy about the recovery process he had gone through. He would listen attentively and gradually insinuate himself into Jimmy's life before he made any reference to the money. If there was a substantial amount which was readily available, he would devise a plan to get a share for himself.

As the working day drew to an end, the warehouse manager came to check on them. He was pleased with their work and he checked with Jimmy that Martin had done his fair share. Jimmy confirmed that he had and, after delivering his broad smile, he shuffled away. Martin made a comment, not directly to the manager, that he had been humbled by Jimmy's resilience and work ethic.

"Do you want to work with him tomorrow?" he was asked.

"Yes, that would be great," said Martin.

He would have to play the long game with Jimmy, Martin decided. Trust and friendship would have to be established. Also, he was still on probation.

The next day at work, Martin went to the packing area and said sheepishly to Jimmy, "You're working with me again. I hope that's alright?"

He was met by a grin and he went to pick up a large box. Day one: Operation "Jimmy's Compensation Money."

At the end of the week, a paltry sum of money was paid into Martin's basic bank account. He wasn't allowed debit or credit cards for obvious reasons. He couldn't help calling at the bookies on Saturday morning. He had two losses and one win which meant he came out about even. That was good for him. Back at the odious hostel, Martin shut himself in his room, away from drug addicts and criminals, and began to draw up a step by step plan for his new operation.

It was now a regular thing for Jimmy and Martin to work together. Sometimes they worked in silence and sometimes they chatted. Martin had learnt that Jimmy lived in a small flat as he wanted to be independent of his family. He did take his washing back to his mum from time to time and she always sent him home again with homemade pies and meals for him to freeze. When he didn't eat those, he made simple things like beans on toast but he liked to get a takeaway pizza every week. That was his favourite.

Martin told Jimmy that he had made a bad mistake and was sent to prison for it. He was very sorry for what he had done and thought he was reacting to the death of his beloved mother. He spoke about her slowly fading away from cancer and how he had nursed her and given her medicine until the end. For the rest of the day, after the disclosure of his mother's death, Jimmy patted him comfortingly on his arm each time he passed.

The next thing Martin discussed with Jimmy, after four weeks of working together, was how miserable he was living in the hostel.

Jimmy thought for a while about the problem and then beamed his smile and said, "Why don't you come and stay with me?"

Martin thanked him for his kind offer but said he would be okay. He would have to notify his probation officer if he changed address and he didn't want him knowing his business. It would be nice to get out of the hostel occasionally though, he said to Jimmy. Maybe he could visit one evening and they could get some pizza? The big dumb smile was back and Martin knew he had hit his mark.

On Friday evening, Martin arrived at Jimmy's tiny but neat flat bearing two pepperoni pizzas. He also had a bottle of cola, a pack of cards, and a box of matches. He was going to teach Jimmy how to play cards and they would bet on the games with matches. Martin would lose most games for the next few weeks before they began to play for money.

Chapter 23

Robert and his family had returned to America and the school holidays had ended. Dorothea, Penny, and Eve had enjoyed a lovely summer and, as they sat down at Penny's house for their Sunday get together, a question hung in the air. Eve did not want to appear to be too keen, so she waited for one of the others to broach the subject on all of their minds, John, the dinner party guest. They had briefly though about Martin Cole, but they were nervous. If anything happened to him, they would be amongst the suspects.

It was Dorothea who mentioned John first. "We've have had six weeks off and now we must knuckle down and get back to business. There's a bad man out there who needs a visit from Eve."

The other two smiled in relief. They all wondered if the others had gone lukewarm on the idea.

"I'll go to the lock up and get the stuff and we can get back to surveillance." Penny said. She opened the oven door and made a face as they smelt carbon. "I think the chicken is done."

All three women donned their disguises and set off for the town where John Hall lived. It was ninety miles away so they treated it as a day out. They were in Penny's car and the number plate had been doctored not only with the use of insulating tape but also white and yellow sticky backed plastic. Their operation was getting more sophisticated.

They dropped Dorothea and her tartan shopping trolley in the area where John had last been working so that she could roam the streets and try to find him. Penny and Eve headed for

John's house to see if he was at home. The van was not in the drive as they drove past so they headed back toward the place they had left Dorothea. They would also walk around the bungalow strewn area looking for John and then rendezvous with Dorothea after an hour.

After months of frustration, they finally caught a break when they saw his van outside one of the bungalows and a ladder leaning against the wall. The temptation was to go into the home the first chance they got to warn the occupants about Mr Hall but that would mean there would be witnesses. They now knew where he was, allegedly, working and although it did not afford them an opportunity to do the deed at present, it was more information than they had before.

Two days later, as Eve sat at a bus stop across the road from John Hall, wearing the short brown wig and an ugly brown anorak, fortune smiled on them. She had been there half an hour and hadn't seen him do anything except talk on his mobile phone when he decided to go up the ladder. Still talking on the phone, he missed his footing and fell to the ground, his foot dangling awkwardly between two rungs.

Luckily a bus arrived and Eve hopped on it. If she had stayed, surely as a witness she would have been obliged to go and offer assistance and that was the last thing she wanted to do. Eve retired to the cafe where her friends were waiting. She eagerly told them about John's fall and they ran to the car and waited at the end of the road and, temporarily, became ambulance chasers. Dorothea shuffled into accident and emergency and took a seat. After a couple of hours, she saw John on a trolley being wheeled toward the lifts.

There was an urgent need to know what had happened. Dorothea couldn't wait and hope, action was needed. Her heart in her mouth, she grabbed her opportunity. She barged her way in with her trolley and peered at the hapless builder. "What you done darling?" she asked in a very Caribbean accident.

The patient just looked at her with contempt.

The nurse accompanying him made the reply. "Bad break of the ankle. He'll need an op and then back home to recover."

"Poor man," said Dorothea shaking her head.

The other two praised Dorothea's initiative in finding out about John's injury. He would be stuck at home after the operation, either unable to move or severely restricted. Penny and Eve would take over the duties now and keep watch on his house until he returned. It meant a lot of travel each day, but they were prepared to do it to get their man. Once he was back, they could see what visitors he got and make a plan from there. He left hospital and was wheeled into his house by a hospital worker four days later. He was in plaster and had been given a pair of crutches.

Over the next few days, he had a couple of callers. One of his lady friends arrived with a bag of groceries and stayed for an hour then left. Another woman came around the next night and brought a bottle of scotch with her. Eve and Penny now travelled with the killing kit in the car. They never knew when their opportunity might come and they wanted to be ready. Because of his size and the threat John Hall posed, it had been agreed that this would have to be a two man, or woman, job. Penny had run up a second coverall in the same fabric and would be armed with the gun. She would threaten him with it while Eve got to work.

After her initial reticence, Penny had become eager to get involved with one of the operations. The size of John Hall meant that he posed a high risk. If tiny Eve tried to tackle him, and he fought back, she would stand no chance. Penny would get to go into the house and point the gun at the big brute. She had secretly practiced producing the gun with a flourish and pointing it as she stood, feet apart, ready for action. It was a shame that she would be dressed in the green leafy onesie when her moment came.

It was a Friday evening when a group of three men arrived at John's house each carrying a large pack of lager. Eve and Penny looked at each other and grinned. When his friends left the house, which hopefully they would, after a drinking session, they would take their chance. They would have to make themselves scarce for a couple of hours until it was fully dark. Later, they would slip into the back garden of the house with their bags and change into the romper suits. The garden was overgrown and would provide concealment while they waited for the all clear.

The timing was difficult for this operation. The ladies had to wait till it was dark to get into the back garden but not run into John's friends as they left his house. They decided to err on the side of caution and go into the garden between nine and ten o'clock. They may have a long wait in the cold, but there was a pay off at the end. Hopefully, their discomfort would lead to the death of the dinner party guest.

***

The lads had come around and brought some beer. Thank God for that. John was utterly bored of being stuck at home. He was in quite a bit of pain too so the alcohol would be most welcome. There were lots of laughs that evening as the friends swapped outrageous stories of past fights and women they had known. John told the boys how he had two girlfriends at his beck and call and that they were visiting bearing gifts and he didn't mean grapes. They all laughed raucously as they bandied sexual innuendo back and forth.

As each lager was finished, the empty cans were dropped onto the floor. One of the women would clear them up on their visit. As more and more beer was consumed, John couldn't remember which one of his ladies was next on the roster. He called them both darling so that he wouldn't use the wrong name and have to explain his mistake. His pain was fading, he was feeling tired, and the drink was running low. It had been good fun but he was glad when his friends decided to leave. He settled back in his recliner chair and began to doze off, content in his drunken haze.

***

John Hall was the eldest of three brothers. He had bullied and beaten up his younger siblings on a regular basis throughout their childhoods but had still been fond of them. He had recruited them to work for his building business and they were happy to do two hours work a day and get paid for eight. They never asked about the work, or lack of it, but they weren't stupid. They knew that John was overcharging customers who were vulnerable for work they didn't need.

When a relative of one of the victims made a complaint to the police. An appeal in the media had brought more of his victims forward. All of his previous customers were contacted and the evidence against him was soon insurmountable. His brothers turned on him then, the bastards, and he took the fall. The truth was that his brothers had become aware of the huge amounts John made and were exacting their revenge for not receiving a larger cut.

He had been abandoned again. First his wife, the moaning cow, who had been unable to give birth to anything but girls and, now, his brothers. There was an upside to everything though. He didn't have to see the daughters who should have been sons anymore and now, he didn't have to share any money he made with anyone else. It was just so easy to con these people. Okay, some of them rumbled him, but nothing ventured, nothing gained. His life since he left prison wasn't so bad. He made decent money and he had a couple of girlies to keep him company when he wanted it.

John's accident was inconvenient; it stopped him earning good money but now he could claim benefits and rest up for a few weeks. The only thing that he had to worry about was ensuring that his girlfriends visited on different days; there would be hell to pay if they ran into each other. All in all, it was a good day.

***

So much relied on fate, if the Gods were with them, they would be able to complete the mission. If not, they should be able to get away. There were so many risks but both ladies were determined to stop this man who had his hooks into another trusting pensioner. As they waited in the shrubbery, they heard the door at the side of the house open and loud voices. Eve moved slightly and saw the three men stagger off back to the road leaving the dinner party guest alone.

They waited for half an hour and, after a quick check of their outfits and equipment was made, Penny and Eve approached the house. Everyone else had walked straight in. It seemed John left the door unlocked. If it was locked, Eve would get a chance to use her lock picking skills. The handle turned and the door opened and they found themselves in the front room of the house looking at John who was snoring in his recliner chair.

Eve carefully closed the door behind them and they crept towards the guest. They froze in the middle of the room when John opened his eyes and stared straight at them. He laughed and waved at them.

"Two leprechauns." He chuckled.

Then one of the leprechauns produced a gun and pointed it at him. His focus was entirely on the armed leprechaun as he frantically tried to get out of his seat. Penny moved forward and aimed the gun at his head. John raised his hands toward her as if to ward her off and it was at this moment that Eve calmly applied the surgical stab to his neck from behind.

As the blood spurted from his neck, John Hall didn't gurgle. He made a slight high-pitched squeal which sounded so bizarre emanating from such a big man. Eve looked at Penny who was leaning over the dinner party guest having a good look. She pointed toward the door and they made their way out clomping in their too large shoes. They made a quick scan around them as they left to check that they hadn't left any footprints and then retreated to the garden.

Once they changed clothes, the ladies donned their disguises and wandered off down the road arm in arm. There were no CCTV cameras on the back streets and they figured slow and steady was less likely to attract attention than rushing away. It was gone one o'clock in the morning and they didn't see anyone on the trip back to the car. They left town using a circuitous route and made a steady drive back home.

Eve and Penny relaxed a bit when they got back to the car. Penny rarely ever got to a speed of more than thirty miles per hour so they didn't have to be worried about getting caught on a speed camera. She also had a somewhat dysfunctional inner compass so their route home would be all round the houses.

After a period of silence as they concentrated on getting out of the town, Penny commented on the killing. "I don't know what I imagined but it was much more ordinary than I thought it was going to be. We went in there, you stabbed him whilst I waved a gun, and that was that."

"Thank God it was ordinary," Eve said. "If he had managed to get out of his chair, it could have all gone horribly wrong."

At that point Penny started to giggle.

"What's so funny?" Eve asked.

"I just have this mental picture of big John Hall hopping around his chair in pursuit of two leprechauns."

Eve began to smile. "Speeded up like a chase in an old silent film." The two of them laughed for the rest of the journey.

It was three o'clock by the time the ladies got home to Eve's house. It was easier to come and go from her home unobserved. They would wait until six thirty and would then go to Dorothea's place to fill her in on the evening's activities. Using mobile phones was out of the question because they could indicate where they were so Dorothea was unaware that they had decided to serve dessert that night. What a nice surprise she would have when they gave her the good news.

Chapter 24

It had been nearly seven months since the last vigilante murder and now it looked as if there had been another one. It was not in their area but Mike and Adam were on their way to the crime scene to assess whether it was similar to the other two cases and, if so, they would liaise on this new one as well. Maybe by cross referencing all the information on the three murders, a suspect would be revealed.

They were summoned when the victim was identified as a convicted conman named John Hall. He was stabbed in the neck. The forensics team were inside in their white suits searching for any evidence. Neighbours said he had been visited by some friends on the Friday night and there were empty beer cans littering the floor which confirmed that.

One of John's girlfriends found the body on Saturday afternoon. She apparently ran around the house in a state of panic looking for his phone as her phone had a flat battery. The crime scene was trampled through further when she went to get someone from next door who also went in to take a look as he made the emergency call.

As the scene of crime officers left the house, Mike asked them if they found anything. There was one footprint in the garden, indistinct again and about a size nine. What was it with the single footprints? The team collected cans and fingerprints and fibres but a door to door revealed that a number of people, including hospital staff, had been in and out of the building as well as the girlfriend and the neighbour, so it was not going to be easy to find a good piece of evidence.

Mike spoke to the Chief Inspector of the neighbouring area on the phone and confirmed that it appeared to be another murder by the, so called, Vigilante Killer. The results of all tests and all the statements taken so far from the other residents of the area would be forwarded to him so they could compare it to the other cases. As they drove back to the police station, Mike said a prayer in his head asking that, this time, the killer had made a mistake.

Dean Robertson read about the murder of John Hall and was absolutely delighted. All that worry and the Vigilante Killer had his eye on someone else the whole time. He could go back to leading a normal life which for him meant being able to go down the pub more often to escape from the girlfriend and kids. He would also get away from the dog which never stopped barking.

The board was back in use with a picture of John Hall added alongside Simon Butler and Eddie Stringer. Once again, a long list of suspects with grudges against John Hall was emerging. Most of his victims were elderly and unlikely to be involved but they still had to check them and their families as well as John's family and friends. The names on the long list would be cross referenced with those on the lists compiled for the other two murder victims to see if there was a link.

The families of the previous victims had not featured prominently in their investigations, but John's brothers were high on the list. There had been bad blood between them and John after he was convicted with the help of their testimony. Although they thought all the murders were by the same man, someone could take the opportunity to get rid of an enemy by using a similar method. Each new murder could be a copycat killing.

John's brothers were rounded up and brought in for questioning. It soon became apparent they had nothing to do with his death. They had credible alibis but Mike doubted they would have had the intellect to plan and get away with a murder. John Hall, remarkably, had been the brains behind the con they had perpetrated. His brothers had been bullied by him and they used his prosecution as an opportunity to get him out of their lives.

Their colleagues on the neighbouring force sent statements taken from people in the area and they were awaiting a report from the forensics team. Mike and Adam would interview suspects at the other force's premises so they were staying at a hotel for a few nights rather than travel back and forth. Mike wasn't one for all that male bonding stuff but as he sat at the bar with Adam in the evening, he found himself talking about his ex-wife.

Adam was shown pictures of the cute dark haired Phoebe and listened as Mike talked about how clever and funny she was. Maria had some Italian heritage and Mike had brown hair so their daughter had inherited their hair colour and his wife's brown eyes. As he sipped his next drink, Mike confided in Adam about the search he made on Gavin and the results which had come back.

"You'll keep worrying what he's up to until you find out; when all this calms down, we'll follow him and see what he's doing," Adam offered.

Mike was glad he had shared his burden and touched that Adam had offered to help. Talking about feelings and relationships wasn't easy for him. Some guys would tell him to get over it, but Adam had been sensitive to the problem. He was starting to like his young colleague.

They called it a day and left the bar to catch a few hours' sleep before the forlorn search for their killer resumed. The door to door enquiries had revealed little except some delight that the bully John Hall was dead. Someone thought they had seen two older ladies strolling down a nearby street late at night on Friday but they had been drinking and couldn't remember anything about them. They would put out the usual appeal through the media for anyone who was in the area and might have seen something to come forward in the hope of speaking to the ladies. That is if there were ladies and the time as given by the witness was correct. He gave unreliable a whole new meaning.

The press reported the shock of another body being found and the danger of there being a serial killer on the loose. The name Vigilante Killer was now firmly entrenched and the police had started using the term as well. Mike read the latest article and couldn't help feeling that the media were secretly thrilled that another murder had been committed so they could fill their columns with stories of the victims' crimes and speculate wildly about who was responsible. At least the people who had been conned were able to sell their stories and recoup some of their losses.

The only thing different about this killing was the fact that there had not been a recent article about John Hall in any papers or magazines. Searches revealed that a magazine had featured a piece about him four years before but that was the only mention they could find.

Mike looked at Adam and said what they were both thinking. “I think our killer saw the article in the paper. The link between stories and murders has been discovered. He changed his method to throw us off the scent and it worked. We have no idea now who he will target next.”

They ploughed on through the paperwork and finally the forensics came back. There was DNA everywhere but most of it had been matched with friends and acquaintances of John Hall. The sequences which remained unmatched were not in their database. They would keep these results in the hope they could identify a suspect who had the same DNA. Lots of things had been bagged at the scene. There was fluff and loose change and paperwork. That which could be tested for fingerprints or DNA had been processed and nothing was conclusive. A single strand of green cotton had been bagged. Why did they bother collecting that, thought Mike?

Adam and Mike were joined by the Chief Inspector and most of the other detectives in front of the board for a brainstorming session.

"The fact that all these people were featured in magazines means that the Vigilante Killer could be just that, a man who has read about these criminals and decided to do something about it," The inspector observed.

"I think you're right," said Mike. "What we have to consider now is what triggered him to act. Was he a victim of a similar type of crime? Maybe a member of his family was conned."

The thought was interesting but would bring them no closer to finding who their killer was. The telephone rang and the impromptu meeting broke up when Adam answered the phone. "There's been another one."

The latest murder had taken place two hundred and fifty miles to the north. A loan shark was killed in his own home by a single stab to the neck.

"What do you think?" Adam asked.

Mike thought for a minute and replied that this time they would wait for a report from the local force rather than travel up there. "It's a long way and too soon after the last one. I was wondering if we were going to get any copycats. This might be one."

Chapter 25

The morning after John the dinner guest had been served his dessert, Penny and Eve sat at Dorothea's kitchen table drinking tea. It was far too early for alcohol they had decided, being only seven o'clock in the morning. Eve had to go to work that Saturday so she would be leaving at eight and was eager to tell all before she had to go.

Penny and Eve told how they spotted the opportunity to strike when they saw John Hall's friends going into the house laden with lager.

"We couldn't phone you because that would have left a trace so we made ourselves scarce for a couple of hours and then went back."

Eve took up the tale. "When we saw them leave, we knew our chance had come. The door was unlocked and we walked straight into the lounge and he was sitting in his chair facing us."

Dorothea clasped her hands to her face as she listened.

"We thought he was asleep but then he opened his eyes and looked straight at us." Penny giggled and then quoted John, "He said 'Two leprechauns' and then waved at us."

Dorothea whispered, "Oh my God."

They described how John had tried to get out of his recliner with his broken ankle and how Penny had pointed the gun at him. Another "Oh my God" escaped from Dorothea's lips.

The gun had the desired effect and John Hall sank back into his chair and as Penny closed in on him, Eve slipped around behind him. As the victim stretched his arms out to defend himself from the advancing gunwoman, Eve plunged the knife into his neck.

"Blood spurted out of his neck like a fountain," Penny said gleefully. "And then he sort of squeaked, and slumped, and that was that."

Again, they didn't make any phone calls because of the late hour and how odd that would look but arranged to meet at Dorothea's the next morning to give her the good news. Another murder had been committed and added to the legend of the Vigilante Killer.

As the tale unfolded, Dorothea felt a pang of jealousy that Penny got to be present for the murder and told her friends how she felt. "I feel a bit left out now. You have both seen the bad guy die."

Eve laughed, "I thought you were too squeamish to take part."

Dorothea considered this. “I am but I still think I’m missing out.”

Eve smiled. “Next time we’ll bring you back the head and you can look at that.”

“No thank you.”

At work after a night with very little sleep, Eve should have been tired but she showed no signs of weariness. The night’s activity had filled her with enthusiasm and she buzzed around her department tidying and offering assistance. She felt fully alert and as though her senses were heightened. It was a long day and, when she finished, she looked back on a good day and night’s work.

On Saturday evening, they met at Eve’s house and watched the reporter intone solemnly about the latest murder by the Vigilante Killer. He described John Hall as a rogue builder and showed pictures of some of the people he had conned. They tracked down his ex-wife and were on her doorstep asking her how she felt about John's death.

She looked at the reporter and said, "I couldn't give a shit." The swear word was bleeped out but one didn't need to be a skilled lip reader to work out what she had said.

***

Tina Hall had finally left her husband after he broke her nose. John would often shout and hurl profanities at her. He would slap her and had directed the odd kick at her. When he threw a punch at her face, she knew it was time to leave. Their three daughters were aged four, two, and one at the time and she knew that she had to get out before they registered what was happening.

Alcohol was usually the fuel for John's anger, but he could be just as mean without it. The thing that he berated his wife for most was that she had not had a son. He took it as a sign of failure or disobedience on her part. He took little notice of the girls and Tina decided they would be better off without him rather than grow up aware of his indifference.

The only things John Hall noticed at home were whether he had clean clothes and whether his dinner was ready. Tina was planning her escape and had been putting the kid's clothes and toys into bags and boxes for a couple of weeks. When John left for work one day, she called a taxi, bundled the girls and her possessions in, and left. John was perplexed when he arrived home after work. Where was everybody, where was his dinner? He couldn't understand why Tina had left him.

She had gone to a shelter for abused women before being housed by the council. Tina spent three years moving from bed and breakfasts to flats and eventually to the house where she now lived. John made contact a couple of times when she first left. He couldn't understand why she had gone. The courts constantly chased him to get the maintenance payments she was due. She had not heard from him directly for years and the girls could not remember him or what he looked like. It was a struggle financially but she and the girls were safe and that was the most important thing.

Later on in the report, some of John's neighbours were interviewed. They talked about a rude, loud, and aggressive man who intimidated people and brought down the area by having piles of junk strewn about his front and back gardens.

Eve nodded as she watched the television. "Yes, the back garden was a mess, but it did provide us with plenty of cover."

They could put it off no longer, Martin Cole would have to be their next dinner party guest. After three murders, they reasoned, killing

Martin would not lead the police to their door. Apparently, another size nine footprint had been left in the garden of John's house so the police were still looking for a lone man.

"Another footprint was found?" Penny wondered where that was discovered.

"Don't worry about it; we had the size nines on," Eve said.

They discussed their retreat from the house and across the rubbish strewn garden and couldn't remember leaving any trace. They made sure that they didn't tread on any patches of soil. That was the trouble with creeping about at night, you couldn't be sure that you had left nothing behind.

The disguises and other paraphernalia were stowed while the ladies investigated the whereabouts of their favourite guest. The temptation was to rush into another operation straight away. This, however, was the most important undertaking of them all and they wanted to get it right.

They managed to wait a couple of weeks before Dorothea asked her son Malcolm if Martin Cole was back in the area, a non-specific question to which he had answered yes. It didn't tell them where he was but it made the search a bit easier. The internet revealed little because the guest had been in prison for the last two and a half years.

"We need to do some lateral thinking," declared Penny.

Her friends looked at her with wonder. Where had that come from. This new dynamic, logical Penny was a revelation.

"If you have just come out of prison and you didn't have family or anybody to stay with, where would you go?"

They ran with this idea and discovered that released prisoners, who were effectively homeless, often went to stay in hostels. There were two in their local area and these would be the focus of the latest surveillance. Disguises were extremely important for this operation as they were known to the guest. A very amusing Sunday afternoon was spent trying on wigs and clothes and adopting different postures and walks to see what worked best. Dorothea's old lady with the trolley would be employed and Penny would wear the curly black wig and the bulky brown anorak.

Carrying out an operation in their home town would make things more difficult. What if one of them was recognised while in disguise by a friend? How would they explain that? "Tell them that you're wearing a wig because all your hair fell out after the shock of the fraud," said Eve. "Let's face we have lost touch with most of our friends. They don't know what to say to someone who has lost so much. They are likely to cross over the road rather than talk to us."

The hostels were in the less pleasant parts of town so they were unlikely to bump into anyone they knew there. They couldn't be put off by risk of seeing someone they knew and they forged ahead with their plan. Early one morning, Dorothea, in her stooped old lady disguise, saw the abhorrent Martin leaving one of the hostels. They now knew where he lived.

Martin set off on foot and Dorothea shuffled a bit quicker and got to the end of the road. Peering around the corner, she saw him waiting at a bus stop. It was seven thirty in the morning. He must be going to work.

"Oh, how the mighty have fallen." Dorothea was reporting back to her accomplices. "Do you remember seeing him drive around town in that red sports car?"

They knew where he was living but the hostel was a busy place, lots of people coming and going throughout the day and into the night. Nothing was going to stop the ladies now though and they spent time watching the place to find a chink in his armour.

Chapter 26

Martin was oblivious to the fact that he was under surveillance. When he left the hostel in the morning, he was still half asleep and, when he returned, he was rushing to get in out of the cold. He earmarked some of the money he got from Jimmy for a thicker coat. He would buy one tomorrow if he could resist laying another bet. He looked at the paper and saw a horse was running that couldn't possibly lose.

Jimmy was so pleased to have a new friend. Martin came to his flat and they drank cola, ate pizza, and, after they had watched some television (Jimmy liked the soaps), they would play cards. The first three weeks, they played for matchsticks. It had taken sometime for Jimmy to grasp how the game worked but by week three, he was winning most of the games they played. As he collected another pile of matches, he would smile his big soppy grin. Martin smiled back as he thought, not long now sucker.

At work, as they packed boxes into boxes, Jimmy and Martin would talk quietly about their Friday night games. Martin said they shouldn't tell their colleagues because they would all want to play and there wasn't enough room in Jimmy's tiny flat; if there were too many of them, they would have to go somewhere else. This was not good for Jimmy, who was only comfortable at work, in his flat, or at his mother's.

Martin spent the first cards night listening to Jimmy talk about his rehabilitation following his accident. He asked lots of questions and showed lots of sympathy. During the second night, Martin asked him about his compensation. Jimmy had received £300,000. His tiny flat had cost £120,000 and the rest was in savings accounts. Martin asked him what he spent his money on and Jimmy replied that he bought clothes, sometimes, and video games.

"If you wanted to buy something big, would you be able to get to your money?" Martin asked.

Jimmy looked somewhat bemused.

"Like a car," Martin had to give him a clue.

"I can't drive because of my injuries."

"Yes, I know Jimmy but that was just an example."

"I can get to my money whenever I want something but I don't want stuff very often," Jimmy said. That was what Martin wanted to hear.

On the fourth games night, as Jimmy tucked into his pepperoni pizza Martin suggested that they play for money instead of matches.

"Then, if you win, you can have pizza every night."

Jimmy liked the idea of that, reflected in his big smile. So they played for money and Martin ensured that Jimmy came out slightly ahead at the end of the evening. This would be the last time he would ever win at cards.

The next week, Martin won twenty-five pounds and Jimmy paid up and confirmed that he was happy to keep on playing every week. Colleagues at work were kind to Jimmy but Martin was the first one to take the time to become his friend and visit him outside of work. The friends that Jimmy knew before the accident had gradually drifted away. Some still called him every now and then but his reluctance to go anywhere outside of his comfort zone made it difficult for him to meet up with them.

Jimmy's mother helped him organise his finances when he moved into his flat. He would get his wages and he knew that he had to put an amount away each week to pay for his bills, gas, electric, council tax, etc. and he had to budget for food as well. After he made sure he covered these expenses, Jimmy had money left which he very rarely spent. He accumulated a couple of thousand pounds in his bank account and that is what he used to pay his gambling debts.

There was an element of discomfort nagging at Jimmy over the amounts he was losing each week but he ignored it because he was so glad to have a friend. He had to remember that Martin bought the pizza and the cola every week; Martin reminded him of this and he didn't complain about watching the soaps. When old friends visited in the past, they didn't realize that it was important to Jimmy to concentrate on his programmes and had talked throughout them.

Now, a couple of months into their regular Friday night games, Martin was winning about one hundred pounds per week. It wasn't a large amount but it supplemented his meagre wages from the food processing plant. Tomorrow, after a small win on the horses as well, he would buy the thicker coat. He wasn't allowed to smoke inside the hostel so he had to go to the small yard at the back of the building. The staff optimistically referred to the yard as the garden but it was just a concrete area with a few overgrown bushes around the edge.

Just one good win, that was what Martin needed, and then he could move out of his dreary room and find somewhere of his own. To lay more bets, he needed more money so he was going to have to start squeezing Jimmy a bit harder. It was important to keep Jimmy interested in the game so this time he would let Jimmy get ahead throughout the evening and would then win a big amount on the last game.

Martin was, of course, cheating when they played cards. It helped that Jimmy had only a tenuous grip on how the game was played. He was alright with pairs and three and four of a kind, that was straightforward. It was when it came to flushes and runs that Jimmy could easily get confused. Martin always dealt the cards because it took Jimmy too long so it gave him the chance to manipulate the hands they received.

He left Jimmy's flat the following Friday having won five hundred pounds from his hapless colleague. A couple more weeks of this and he might even have saved enough for a deposit on a rented home. Of course, he might use the money to lay bets if he saw a good horse was running. A couple weeks later, Jimmy lost again and had no more money in his bank account. When he took his washing to his mum's house, he asked her if he could have some of his savings. He hadn't mentioned to Martin that his mother controlled the access and he had to ask her first.

Chapter 27

The ladies had been watching the hostel where Martin Cole was living for some time and their patience was beginning to wear thin. They wanted to plan carefully for this operation but that was being offset by their eagerness to see the end of him. The only time he was alone was when he was travelling to and from work and when he came home on a Friday night after going out about seven o'clock.

There was probably some kind of curfew at the hostel because Martin returned just after ten o'clock at night. At that time, a number of other people were invariably making their way into the hostel as well. An Eve saw Martin standing outside in the yard smoking a cigarette: an opportunity. Sometimes there were other residents there too but sometimes he was on his own. If he was on his own, he would walk around the concreted area as he smoked.

"This could be the only chance we get." Eve was updating her friends on what she had seen over the last few nights.

"It worries me. There's a high risk of being discovered," Dorothea cautioned.

The pros and cons of the situation were batted back and forth for the next hour before a decision was reached. Killing Martin Cole was the most important thing to all of them so a risk would have to be taken.

Penny and Dorothea were the cautious ones. Eve's determination to carry out the murder made her prone to recklessness. Martin Cole could be alone in the back garden but another resident could join him at any time. It was decided that Eve must wait in the bushes and only strike when Martin walked past close to her. "The last thing you want to do is have to kill someone else as well because they are a witness." Dorothea made Eve think with what she had said.

"That's if you could kill them. Most men could overpower someone of your size," Penny added.

"What do you mean 'of your size'? Are you implying I'm short?" Eve dared Penny to respond.

"You could use the word short or you could say pocket size." Penny was smiling and Eve decided to let it go, having taken their advice on board.

Eve would travel to the area in disguise with her shopping bag, change into her coverall, and secrete herself in the bushes in the back garden. She would wait there for a chance to present itself. If Martin was alone making his sad circuit of the garden, she would strike as he walked past. Should someone turn up in the minutes after the murder, they would have to go for help and she would have a short time to make her escape.

It was a plan fraught with problems. There were so many variables and the danger of being discovered was high. Eve was determined to proceed, however, and Dorothea and Penny only made a token show of trying to talk her out of it. They decided to employ the mobile phone ruse again. Penny would use Eve's phone in Eve's house and the others would make calls from their own houses thereby establishing where they were.

There was a patch of scrubland next to the hostel where Eve found a place to change into her outfit and conceal her bag. She crept from bush to bush and made her way into the backyard through a gap in the fence. After the deed had been done, she would crawl back through the fence onto the scrubland and make her getaway.

As Eve waited in the overgrown bushes, she could hear her heart pounding. This was not like the other murders; this was Martin Cole. A great deal of responsibility was weighing on Eve as she sought revenge for herself, Penny and Dorothea. She would have to act quickly and get away cleanly. She had never been overly concerned about the waiting she had to do before but now she was restless. She had only been there an hour but it felt like three. Adrenalin was coursing through her body as the back door of the hostel opened.

At last, Martin emerged through the back door and lit his cigarette. He was wearing a brand new coat. A coat that Eve hoped would soon be soaked in blood. God, she hated that man. As the door closed behind him, the garden was once more in darkness. True to form, Martin set off for his short walk around the yard and Eve felt every muscle in her body tense as she prepared to pounce.

Then the door opened again, a shaft of light broke the gloom, and a skinny youth appeared saying “Alright mate.” Eve was taken by surprise and took a step backwards making the bushes move.

Eve froze as Martin and the youth turned their attention to the area of the garden in which she was hiding. Martin returned to the back of the building and stood next to the other man.

“What was that?” he asked.

“Just a fox or a cat mate.” The young man grinned. “What did you think it was, the Vigilante Killer? Don’t worry, mate, he only goes after fraudsters.”

Martin fixed the man with a frightened stare and finally made the admission, out loud and to himself. “I am a fraudster.”

The cigarette in Martin’s hand was shaking as he realised that he might be the type of person who would be of interest to the Vigilante Killer. The skinny youth was busy smoking and talking about his nefarious past. Martin vaguely heard something about drugs and burglaries; he could have guessed that but he was now desperate to get back into the hostel where he would be safe. He threw his cigarette butt on the floor and stamped it out before beating a hasty retreat.

Martin and his new friend went back into the building and Eve could move at last. She had managed to get into a crouching position behind the bush and her muscles were burning with the effort of staying still. She made a very careful exit through the fence to the place where she had hidden her bag. A quick change back into a disguise, heading off through back roads, and back to Dorothea's house where the girls were waiting. As she returned, she had to sit down at a bus stop for a while and calm herself. Eve let herself in and Penny and Dorothea jumped up from their seats expectantly. The look on their friend's face told them all they needed to know.

The kettle was put on and Eve told them about the close call in the yard at the back of the hostel.

"I was ready. He was there. And then some bloke came out. I had to back off and he heard me, got all nervous and rushed back in. I was so close."

"We won't be able to catch him there now; he's been spooked," observed Penny.

"Thank goodness you weren't caught. At least we are free to try a new plan," Dorothea said.

"I can't believe that other guy actually joked that it was the Vigilante Killer. That has probably put him on his guard. More surveillance and more planning I'm afraid." Eve looked at the ladies who nodded their agreement.

They had got away with it so far but they needed to take more care. They didn't want to be caught at all but if they were, they wanted to go down with the knowledge that Martin Cole was no more. It had always been risky approaching him at the hostel where so many people were coming and going. They would have to bide their time and wait for a better opportunity to present itself.

The rest of the night, the women were subdued. They decided to take a few days off to rest and recharge their batteries and then meet up again for their usual Sunday lunch. Penny and Eve left Dorothea's house and set off in opposite directions to their own homes. All of them went to bed that night disappointed but with a determination to find a way to complete the mission.

Chapter 28

Martin Cole couldn't get back into the hostel fast enough after hearing that sound in the bushes. The annoying youth that had come outside to smoke may have just saved his life. He hurried upstairs to his room and locked the door once he was inside. He needed to go to the bathroom and had to pluck up the courage to leave his room, run down the hall, and then run back again afterward.

He hardly slept that night. What if someone was out there waiting for him? He could have been murdered by the Vigilante Killer. By the time morning arrived, Martin had convinced himself that someone was out to get him. He telephoned his work and told them he had to go for an urgent appointment and would be in late. Half an hour later, he was walking into the police station and demanding to talk to whoever knew about the Vigilante Killer.

He had no love of the police, but that did not stop him seeking their help. Martin did not want to become a victim of the Vigilante Killer and he would demand that they investigate. Panic drove him through the doors of the building before he had time to think about the consequences. All he could think about was saving himself.

The call came from reception advising him that someone wanted to talk to him about the Vigilante Killer. Mike got up wearily from his desk and made his way to the stairs. A number of people had phoned or turned up claiming to know something about the murderer. Some of them genuinely thought they were helping, some were pursuing a personal vendetta by trying to get someone into trouble, and some of them were crazy. It was probably pointless, but he had better see what this person wanted.

After the second murder, there had been a steady stream of people phoning up or calling into the station with information. There were suggestions as to who the killer might be with very few of the so called leads being of any use. Some people were convinced that it was a neighbour or work colleague who was responsible and a surprising number of women thought their husband was the killer. One lady phoned every week with a new name.

This one was different. The man at reception was agitated because he was convinced that he had narrowly escaped being the next victim of the killer. His name was Martin Cole and he had recently been released from prison after serving time for fraud. Mike took him to an interview room and sent for Adam to join him.

When they were settled, Mike asked Martin to tell him exactly what had happened.

The story of the noise in the bushes in the back garden of the hostel was a little underwhelming. Adam asked if he had gone to investigate.

"Would you wander off into some bushes if you thought a killer was lurking there?" Martin asked.

That was a fair point but, as the other person who was with him had said, it could have just been an animal. Martin did seem very disturbed by what had happened so they took his statement and then went off to discuss this development.

"The thing is, he matches the profile of the type of person the Vigilante Killer would target. It was probably just a cat or something, but now that he's been brought to our attention, we should follow this up."

Adam agreed. They went back into the room and offered to carry out covert surveillance on Martin so they could see if anyone was hanging around his home or place of employment.

Back in the interview room, the recollection of the last time he had been in a place like this had had a sobering effect on Martin. He never imagined himself voluntarily going to a police station. He began to think about the incident and tried to convince himself that it was nothing sinister. It was almost certainly an animal he had heard in the bushes. Coming here to the police, he was inviting them to look into his life and he was worried about what they would find relating to his dealings with Jimmy. He took a few deep breaths and resolved to apologise to the police for wasting their time and get the hell out of there.

The detectives went back to Martin but before they could talk to him about their plan, he stood up and started sidling towards the door.

"I've been thinking about it and it must have been an animal. I don't know what I was thinking coming here and making a fuss. I can see now I was just being paranoid. I think we can forget about all of this."

Mike and Adam looked at each other, mystified by the sudden change in Martin's attitude.

He was ushered back into his seat by Mike who then suggested that they keep an eye on him to see if he was being targeted. Martin was horrified. His carefully laid plans with Jimmy, which were starting to pay off, would be ruined if he was followed. He smiled at the detectives as he desperately thought of something to say which would stop them.

"I appreciate the offer but forget it. You are right. It was probably just a cat or a fox. All this talk of the Vigilante Killer has made me paranoid."

He went to work and came home at rush hour and the rest of the time, he was in a crowded hostel, Martin explained. He reported regularly to his probation officer so he would inform him if he had any further concerns. The probation officer would liaise with them if anything else happened.

They let him go but they didn't need his permission to drive down his road or sit outside the hostel. Their surveillance would go ahead without his knowledge. Mike spoke to the chief inspector and a couple officers were enlisted to help with observation. Maybe this was it. Maybe this was the breakthrough they had been waiting for. They were briefed on what to look for, a white man in his thirties, hanging around the hostel.

Over the next week, the police drove past the hostel or sat in a car at the corner of the road watching to see if anyone suspicious was frequenting the area. The hostel was busy with a seemingly endless turnover of people coming and going. The residents were all identified and signed in and signed out so they were not under suspicion. At no time did they notice anyone watching the hostel.

It was beginning to look like another pointless exercise. They weren't picking up anything suspicious and then Martin spotted the car. He approached and rapped on the window. Mike wound the window down and delivered his charming smile. Another annoying smiler, thought Martin. He was not pleased about the police presence. He spouted some angry remonstrations about his civil liberties being infringed and advised that he would be contacting his solicitor.

“We are only looking out for your safety.” Mike tried that out as an excuse but it was not going to work. Martin Cole was very angry. He made it quite clear that if he saw them again, he would sue for harassment.

When they got back to the station, they were, once again, despondent.

“How can we be harassing him if we’re trying to save his life?” Adam asked.

They reviewed the operation and the lack of any results and had to concede defeat. They had not seen anyone suspicious hanging around the hostel or as Martin entered and left work. A decision about carrying on the operation was due to be made soon and this had brought it to a head.

“Write it all up in case he gets himself killed and this whole thing comes back to bite us in the arse,” Mike advised.

As Eve wandered down the road next to the hostel, she glanced into the car at the end of the road and recognised the handsome detective from the television. She strolled on unhurried and then made her way home. She was in disguise, the short brown wig and horrible anorak, so she wasn't overly concerned. If they were watching Martin Cole, they were looking for a man but they would have no choice but to back off for the time being.

"You're sure it was him." Dorothea was concerned with what Eve had reported about seeing the detective near the hostel.

"Absolutely sure. Dark hair, lovely blue eyes, it was him. We have to back off for a while just in case."

There was no dissent from the group. Eve had told them her theory about why the police were near Martin's place of residence and why they had barely noticed her. She thought that they were looking for the Vigilante Killer.

“Maybe they are watching him because he is involved in another con.” Penny made them all think with that comment.

They had ridden their luck for a while now and, whatever the reason for the surveillance, they didn’t want to push it any further. Their time would come but that time was not now.

***

Martin checked the street every time he left the hostel now. He was more worried about the police discovering his activities than he was about the Vigilante Killer. He hoped that his tirade had worked and that they backed off. He was particularly careful when he left the hostel on Friday nights to visit Jimmy. Nobody needed to know about that. After a few days, it appeared that they had heeded his warning of legal action and he began to relax again.

***

As usual, at the end of the day, Adam and Mike stood in front of the board with the three photographs pinned at the top and waited for something to reveal itself that would crack the case open. A nd per usual, they walked away after a few minutes none the wiser. Hopefully Phoebe would work her magic this weekend and Mike would return to work on Monday with his hope and determination restored.

Chapter 29

The murder which had taken place in the north was turning out to be exactly what they thought it was, a copycat killing. A neighbour of the victim had seen a man entering and leaving the house around the time of the murder and a car was caught on CCTV before and after the killing as well. The number plate on the car had led them to a man who was known to the loan shark and he had been apprehended and questioned.

It was a sorry tale of a man who had run up a huge debt which he could not repay and, in desperation, he had hatched an ill conceived plan to kill the loan shark and make it look like the Vigilante Killer. The victim in this case got less sympathy than the perpetrator. But he had gone there with a plan and that made it murder.

***

Paul Sims was in a terrible mess. He had borrowed a small amount, £300, from a loan shark and, at first, he had made the weekly repayments of twenty pounds. He lost his job and then had to wait for his benefits and went into arrears. Twenty pounds a week seemed such a small amount but now that he had fallen behind, he was beginning to panic. One of the repayment collectors had made veiled threats when he was unable to pay.

The tiny debt was growing at a rapid rate and had already reached four figures after only a couple of months. As he missed more repayments, he was advised that the debt had reached over three thousand pounds and that, if he didn't hand over some money soon, he would get a visit which would remind him how unhappy they were with the situation.

He could see no way out. Paul was out of his mind with worry and risked everything. He, like virtually everybody else in the country, had read about the Vigilante Killer and his murders where the victims were stabbed in the jugular vein. Grabbing a knife, he set off in his car and killed the loan shark. There had been no carefully laid plan. Paul was crazy with worry and that would form the basis of his defence.

***

Their fellow detectives, from the area of the crime, reported the news and asked Mike and Adam how they felt about hunting for someone who, in essence, was doing them all a favour. They had been keen to catch the loan shark killer but when they heard his story of woe, they could sympathise with him. Many people in the town had been elated by the killing and regarded the murderer as a local hero.

Alibis had been provided for the times of the other killings which no one seriously thought he had committed. Mike and Adam were grateful they hadn't had to make the long journey to the scene of the crime for a murder that was not linked to their killer. Their killer would not have been as sloppy as to be seen by a witness or be caught on camera.

The press sadly reported that the loan shark killing wasn't linked to the Vigilante Killer but then gleefully advised that the culprit had been found. It gave them an excuse to rehash all they knew about the previous murders and the victims and to wonder speculatively why no one had been apprehended. Mike sat and read an article about the nature of serial killers which speculated about the profile of the person they would be searching for.

Mike read the informative piece about serial killers and what the police profile might say. All of the serial killers in fact and fiction seemed to be Caucasian males aged between twenty and thirty who had tortured animals and been subjected to physical or sexual abuse as children. These myths were debunked one by one.

Certain traits were prevalent in people who became serial killers. A high percentage showed psychopathic tendencies and had been abused as children but this was not always the case. Psychopaths were people who often felt little emotion because their brains were wired differently. They showed intolerance which could then lead to violence. Psychopaths appeared uncaring but were accomplished liars and generally viewed themselves as better than everyone else.

Some serial killers had tortured or killed animals as children but many had not. There were theories that the children of alcoholic parents became murderers due to damage sustained whilst in the womb. The picture in many peoples' minds when they heard the words serial killer was of a loner, a social misfit. Some of them, however, were charming and popular and had families. They were hiding in plain sight.

Another myth was that the killers were generally white. If the victims were white, it was likely that the killer would come from the same racial group. Serial killers came from all ethnic backgrounds. What motivates them was interesting but wasn't necessarily helpful for catching them. Mike scanned the reasons and hit upon the word ideology. This related to his killer who was ridding the world of criminals.

The style of the murder was of consequence. An organised execution of the crime tended to indicate that the perpetrator was of higher intelligence and may be older. They would likely be in a stable job and have friends and families. A more frenzied approach could be attributed to someone with a mental problem, like schizophrenia.

Whilst a lot of murders were carried out by friends and family of the victim, serial killers were not usually known to their victims; this made catching them difficult. The police often had to wait for the killer to become overconfident and make a mistake. Jeffrey Dahmer had been caught when one of his intended victims escaped and was able to identify him. Dahmer, otherwise known as the Milwaukee Cannibal, murdered sixteen men and boys. He cannibalised some parts of their bodies and tried to preserve other parts.

Luck also played a part in the catching of murderers. Ted Bundy had been caught when he had been pulled over for a routine traffic stop and a body was found in the boot of his car. After ten years of imprisonment and shortly before his execution, Bundy confessed to murdering thirty women over a four year period in the 1970's. It is thought that the actual number of killings would be much higher.

The article observed that there were very few women serial killers and went on to deliver its profile of the Vigilante Killer as provided by a retired police officer. The killer would be a white male, aged between thirty and forty. He was organised and careful so he would likely be working and could even have a family. He was killing for an ideological reason. The victims were bad people. Whether he was a psychopath or was abused as a child was hard to tell, but would not be established until, or if, he was caught. Mike looked at the profile which had been produced by their police expert and there were many similarities with the one in the paper.

The ladies also read the article and were delighted with the profile that the newspaper had given.

"So, they're looking for a white, middle aged man." Eve grinned at the other ladies.

"With size 9 feet." Penny said.

"I think our police are wonderful, but I'm really glad that they are completely wrong this time." Dorothea said.

"It's a bit disturbing, all those things they say about us. Well, serial killers." Penny commented.

"The article says they are intelligent, I like that bit. Also, that they can have friends and family and lead normal lives. I don't think any of us have tortured animals? No, good. And the bit about psychopathic tendencies only applies to Eve." Dorothea waited for Eve's reaction to that, but a raised eyebrow was all that was forthcoming.

Martin Cole read the article because, despite what he had told the police, he was worried that he may be on the Vigilante's to do list. He took something very different away from the piece that he studied. The description of a psychopath could have been a description of him. He was uncaring, his mother's illness had annoyed him, he was selfish, a superb liar, and he was better than everyone else. He had never been violent but he was sure he would be capable of it should the need arise. If he found that killer loitering around him, for example.

The police were off Martin's back now and he felt more relaxed about relieving Jimmy of his compensation money. He had gone easy on him last week just winning fifty pounds as he had noticed that his mark was getting a bit jumpy. This week, normal service would be resumed and Martin was hoping to walk away with a couple of hundred pounds at least. He thought about his actions for a moment and then laughed. Just like the article described, he didn't care about what he was doing or worry about Jimmy's feelings.

Chapter 30

The article in the newspaper about serial killers was the exception, in that it was well written and informative. The majority of the reports on the Vigilante Killer were of a more sensational nature. The press had got more excited after the third murder and a number of people who had been dragged into the scams of the victims were now being given their fifteen minutes of fame.

Patricia, the unfortunate woman conned by Simon Butler, was interviewed by one of the tabloids. She was pictured staring sadly at the camera dressed in a designer dress sat on a massive leather sofa. It seemed that Patricia still had some money left after her encounter with Simon and did not evoke much sympathy.

Another paper countered with an interview with Simon's mother. She was much better for sales. Her abject apologies for her son's actions and her confession of the part her and her husband had played in turning him into the selfish, lazy man he had become were lapped up by the public. Each time Simon Butler's name was mentioned by the press, it was followed by the words "a convicted fraudster." No one was allowed to forget his crimes.

The police were amazed at the number of women who came forward with stories about Simon Butler when the newspapers waved some money around. They had desperately tried to find more of his victims when they were building a case against him. The women they could find had been reluctant to admit that they had been duped and certainly didn't want their mistakes revealed to the public during a trial. Their qualms had disappeared when they were tempted by cheque book journalism.

Eddie Stringer's stories were even more lurid thanks to the fact that he had lived with Justine. The photographs of her in all the papers were not of a demure grieving woman. She was in various stages of undress depending on what type of paper she was appearing in. For Justine, it was giving her a chance to get back in the public eye. She was a bit annoyed that she had to keep talking about Eddie. It was not good for her image to be associated with the fat slob. Still, it had let her have a second bite of the fame cherry. She had even booked a reality show which was paying rather well.

Poor Mr. and Mrs. Brook were paraded in the paper again, once more telling their story about how they lost money to Eddie's boiler room scam. Most people hoped that they were paid for their story. Following the report, they had received money through the post from strangers who had read about them. It was a bit embarrassing but they couldn't afford to reject peoples' charity. They still looked sad in the photograph that accompanied the article. It would have been bad form for them to be smiling at someone's death though, however bad that person was.

One of the tragicomic pieces featured the operation to remove Eddie Stringer's body from the path on which it had been found. The stretcher usually used by the medical examiner was not big enough to carry the corpse. The body bag was not big enough either. The body had to remain where it had been found until specialist equipment could be brought in. The paper said that a health and safety assessment had to be carried out before he could be moved.

When John Hall was described in newspaper articles along with "convicted fraudster," the words "Thug" or "cowboy builder" or "wife beater" were also used. The fact that he had been seeing two women at the same time, neither of whom knew about the other, was exploited shamelessly by the press. Each of the ladies were featured in stories in which they claimed to be the love of John's life and insults, of a highly of a personal nature, were thrown back and forth.

It was appalling, really, to see the two women trying to out-grieve one another. One would appear clutching a cheap trinket that John had bought for her, dressed in black with a tear stained face. A couple of days later, the other woman would be pictured holding a blown up photograph of him next to her heart as she dabbed at her eyes with a handkerchief. The two women couldn't believe their luck at being featured in the press.

The spectacular end to the feud occurred when both ladies attended John Hall's funeral. They got into a fight in the car park of the crematorium and the papers gleefully printed photos of hair pulling, punches being thrown, and the women rolling on the ground. The press had pitted these women against each other and was ready with their telephoto lenses to catch the drama when the two ladies finally met. They were eventually pried apart and each of them had a policeman stood next to them during the service in case they kicked off again.

Many journalists tried to get a quote from John's ex wife who was as taciturn as ever. She had gotten rid of him and hadn't seen him for many years. When asked what her daughters felt about their father's death she said, "They don't care; they didn't even recognise him in the photo in the paper." She followed that with some choice words saying where they could go and how they could get there. The statement about her daughters was sad but true.

Every story included a picture of Detective Inspector Mike Nash. He was very photogenic. He couldn't go anywhere now without someone recognising him. The press phoned the station constantly wanting to talk to him and get updates on the investigation. It was quickly decided that the standard response would be that no further information was available at that time. The journalists still phoned though.

The more serious newspapers were asking questions about why the crime hadn't been solved. The others were trying to turn the Vigilante Killer into a folk hero. He murdered people and that was bad but he had put an end to the criminal careers of people who caused heartbreak and ruin. A moral debate was raging and the victims of fraud crimes and the general public appeared to be on the side of the killer.

Eve, Penny, and Dorothea read the press coverage with great interest. The friends now read everything they could to see what else the police had discovered. The whole tone of the reporting had evolved since the first murder of Simon Butler.

The outrage at the murders had now been replaced by a growing admiration for the Vigilante Killer. The ladies marvelled at the change in the perception of the murders by the press and the public. The papers were just about stopping short of glorifying the work of the Vigilante Killer. They always finished their articles by condemning the killings after they had talked about the terrible crimes the murder victims committed.

"Who'd have thought we would end up as heroes?"

Dorothea was reading an article about the murder of John Hall which appeared under the heading "Another one bites the dust." It said that he would no longer be able to con vulnerable pensioners and that there would be one less criminal for the police and courts to deal with.

"It's always nice to be appreciated when you have done a good job," Eve said, smiling.

"It's frustrating that no one will ever know it was us," Penny commented. Eve and Dorothea turned to look aghast at their friend. "Obviously we don't want to get caught but you know what I mean."

Simon Butler, Eddie Stringer, and John Hall were not worthy of anyone's sympathy. That was the general consensus. The fraudsters in the area were looking over their shoulders. Most of them would carry on with what they were doing but if this campaign of retribution put a couple of them off, that would be a bonus. As one headline said, "Which scumbag will be next?"

Chapter 31

Jimmy would often tell people that he wasn't normal following his accident. He had suffered brain damage and was not that clever but he knew deep down that he should not be handing all that money over to Martin. The quandary was, if he stopped paying, would he lose his only friend? He was going to his mother's home to get some washing done and collect some food for his freezer. He would have to ask her for some of his compensation money which was in a special account that she managed.

After the accident, Jimmy's mother Jane had been reluctant to let him go off and live on his own. His brain damage left him childlike and she worried about his capability to look after himself and make decisions. She would not, however, be around forever to care for him and letting him go would prepare him for the future. He came back regularly for visits and help so she could keep an eye on him without being an overbearing mum.

When he arrived, Jimmy seemed agitated. He followed Jane around the house and when they went to the kitchen and his mother put the kettle on, he stood next to the table instead of sitting in his usual place.

"You obviously have something on your mind Jimmy. Why don't you sit down and tell me about it?"

Jimmy pulled out a chair and slumped into it. His mother said nothing and waited for him to muster his thoughts and tell her what the problem was.

"I need some of my compensation money," Jimmy announced whilst staring at the floor.

He knew that his mother was going to ask him why. She did ask him and he said that it was for his friend, Martin.

"Who is Martin and why are you giving him money?" she demanded.

Jimmy took a deep breath and revealed that Martin was a friend from work and that they had been playing cards on Friday nights. Jimmy had lost for the last few weeks and had spent all the money in his bank account and now needed some more.

Jane was appalled at what she heard and sank into a chair next to Jimmy. All her fears had become manifest. Someone had, quite deliberately, targeted and taken advantage of her son. She looked at Jimmy and saw that he was close to tears. He had thought something was wrong and the look on her face must have confirmed it. She calmly told Jimmy that she didn't think it was a good idea to play cards with Martin any more.

"But he brings me pizza and coke."

"Do you remember when I told you that not all people are kind? The rest of your work mates have been nice to you but I don't think that this Martin is a good man. He is cleverer than you and he has most likely cheated at cards to get you to give him money." As Jane explained what had been happening, Jimmy started to cry. "I think you knew it wasn't right but didn't want to tell anyone." Jimmy nodded miserably.

"He's not really my friend then"

"No, he's not."

***

Jane's marriage, already rocky, had broken under the stress resulting from Jimmy's accident. Her husband kept in contact with Jimmy and her but now lived in another part of the country. She would have to tackle this Martin on her own. She wasn't sure that he had done anything illegal but it was certainly immoral. Jane decided that she would be present the next day, a Friday, when Martin arrived and would tell him that she would call the police if he ever contacted Jimmy again. On the following Monday, she would call Mr Evans at the factory and tell him what Martin had been doing. Jimmy was told that he must act like normal at work and carry on with the arrangement.

The next day, Jimmy was on boxes as usual but someone had phoned in sick and Martin was moved to lorry loading. Jimmy had been coached by his mother to say nothing about her knowing about the card games but was nervous of letting it slip. He was thankful that he did not have to talk to Martin much. He was sure he would blush and stammer and end up saying the wrong thing.

As he walked down the road to Jimmy's flat carrying the pizzas and coke, snug in his warm coat, Martin was a happy man. He liked pizza as well and would enjoy that and get some cash too. Jimmy opened the door and, when he stepped in, Martin was met by a woman with a very stern look on her face. It was Jimmy's mother. He tried a winning smile and offered a handshake but he knew he was in trouble.

As he withdrew his hand, the tirade began.

"I know what you have done. You are despicable for exploiting my son in this way. Not only have you stolen Jimmy's money, you have broken his heart by pretending to be his friend. If you so much as look at Jimmy, I will call the police and you can explain your actions to them."

Martin stood straight faced and let Jane rant and rave for a few minutes and, finally, she stopped.

Martin shrugged as if to say, oh well it's a fair cop. He looked Jimmy's mother in the eye and grinned as he said, "It'll be hard not to look at him when we work together."

Jane grinned back. "That won't be an issue for too much longer."

Martin turned around and left the flat still clutching the pizza. He had put the coke down when he went in but that was no great loss. He stomped back to the hostel fuming.

Back at the hostel, Martin ate all the pizza and felt bloated and slightly queasy afterwards. That Jane was going to tell the factory owner what he had done. They would let him go and he would be stuck in this godforsaken place for even longer. He checked the small stash of money he had left and found two hundred pounds. Tomorrow he would go to the bookies and pray for a miracle.

Whichever God Martin had prayed to finally heard his plea. He picked all the winners in his four fold accumulator bet and was looking at winnings in excess of twenty thousand pounds. He would be finding somewhere else to live and looking for a better job. One more suited to his abilities.

Chapter 32

Over the weekend, Martin hand delivered his resignation letter to the chicken factory. He had told Mr Evans, in his brief note, that he did not think he was suited to factory work and that he would not be coming back. He jumped before he was pushed. As Mr Evans took the call from Jimmy's mother, Jane, he was holding the letter in his hand.

He had money in his pocket and was sitting in a letting agent's deciding which property he would rent. Martin decided, in a brief moment of sanity, to pay a deposit and six months' rent in advance. He could then relax, take time to find himself a better job, and make plans for a new moneymaking scheme. He was tempted by the luxury apartments but, in the end, chose a small terraced house. He was sick to death of all aspects of communal living. He wanted his own front door.

The house was furnished with serviceable, if not particularly attractive, items and near to the centre of town. The train station was at the end of the road, which was always busy and noisy and this made it cheap to rent. There was a small garden which had been paved over, at the back and behind that was an alleyway which could be accessed by a gate. He informed his probation officer about his change of address and state of unemployment; he didn't want to break the rules and be sent back to prison and assured him that he would be working again soon.

Martin treated himself to a tablet computer from his winnings and was now sat in a cafe using their wi-fi to search for a job. It would not be a low paid job in a factory this time. He wanted to go to work in his new suit and meet people with money. His eyes read of one vacancy and he found himself saying yes out loud, as he jotted down the details. It was for the position of a double glazing salesperson.

The next day Martin presented himself at the offices of the double glazing company. If he had applied in the usual way, he would not have been given a chance but, in person, he could be very persuasive. He was wearing his new suit and shoes and his hair was neatly trimmed. He shook hands with the boss and said all the right things and left half an hour later having secured the job. He would start the next week by attending a training course, which he doubted was necessary, and then he would go out a couple of times with an existing salesperson before being let loose on his own. He was back.

It was on his second solo visit that Martin secured his first sale for his new employer. He had been relaxed and friendly and was soon enjoying a cup of tea in the clients' house and chatting about family and holidays. Martin noted that their house was awash with souvenirs from all the countries they had visited and started a conversation about travel and was now listening attentively to their many stories. What a nice man, the couple commented, when he left. What an easy sale, Martin thought, and made a note of their details for future use.

Within weeks, Martin was the top salesman and bonuses were coming thick and fast. His colleagues invited him for drinks after work, probably hoping he would be generous with his good fortune but he always declined. He had no use for these people. He was laying the groundwork for his next scam and every client name that was added to his list was another potential victim.

Finally, his probation ended. Martin had hated having to report to his probation officer and answer his inane questions. The stupid man always asked him if he was staying out of trouble. As if he would tell him if he wasn't. Now he could stop thinking about what he might do and start putting his plans into action.

The police had been informed of Martin's change of address and Mike had driven by the terraced house once, out of curiosity. They couldn't follow him or watch him anymore but the detective couldn't help but think that he was exactly the type of person that the Vigilante Killer would target and, despite the fact that he was an unpleasant fraudster, he was concerned that his life was in danger. The surveillance they had carried out on Martin had revealed nothing but now that he was out of the hostel and living alone, he was more vulnerable.

Chapter 33

Adam had found some new coloured whiteboard pens and was rewriting all of their notes beneath the photographs which were pinned at the top of the board. Simon Butler's notes were in blue, Eddie Stringer's were red, and John Hall's were green. He stood back and admired his work. Okay, some of the words were a bit crammed in where he had run out of room but it looked very professional. Unfortunately, it was not going to help them solve the case.

What Adam was doing was pretty pointless but the fact that Mike sat watching him do it was even more so. Mike kept thinking about the lucky policeman who had opened Ted Bundy's car boot and discovered a body and thereby solved a serial killer mystery. He fantasised about being left a crucial clue at the next murder which would lead to the Vigilante

Killer's capture. The downside was that there would have to be another murder for them to find a clue.

He looked at his watch and decided to call it quits. In a couple of hours, he would pick up Phoebe and he could forget about all of this for a couple of days. He said goodbye to Adam, who was still making minor adjustments to his masterpiece, and headed home to change out of his suit. He arrived at his ex-wife's home and was surprised to see a different car in the drive.

Maria opened the door and said that Phoebe was collecting her homework and would be right out.

"Whose car is that?" Mike asked.

"It's mine. Gavin bought it for me," she said, smiling.

The car wasn't brand new; it was five years old but it was very tidy and wouldn't have been cheap. He managed a "that's nice" and then thankfully his daughter appeared and he could leave.

Over the weekend, information was innocently passed on to Mike from Phoebe. They had a new washing machine and were getting a new sofa. Mummy and Gavin were looking at places to go on holiday. There was definitely more money to spend since Gavin had got a new job working nights.

"What is it that Gavin does at his job?" Mike enquired.

"Um, he makes things which are called components." Well, that could mean anything.

After going to the cinema to see the latest animation, Mike took Phoebe for ice cream which was her favourite.

"Why are you frowning, Daddy? Is it because of all the bad people you have to arrest?"

Mike looked at his daughter, face was dappled with strawberry ice cream, and smiled. "I was thinking how cross mummy would be if she saw what you were eating." They both laughed and Phoebe turned her attention back to the large dessert in front of her.

What job making components paid enough money to cause such a change in Gavin's finances? One often earned more working nights, but not that much more. A new car, a new washing machine and sofa and arranging a holiday, that was a lot of expense. Only a couple of months ago, Maria and he had been arguing about money and now they were rolling in the stuff. Gavin had conned people before, was he doing it again?

"How was your weekend with Phoebe?" Adam asked on Monday morning.

"I had to go and see that animated film where they all kept singing, even the animals, but apart from that, it was great. Do you remember that conversation we had about Gavin, my ex's boyfriend? I think we may have to look into that situation before too long." Mike told his colleague about the amount of money he suddenly seemed to have and how suspicious this made him, in light of the previous complaint against Gavin.

Adam nodded gravely. "Just say the word."

Every murder that happened within a two hundred mile radius was now flagged up to Mike and Adam so they could check if it was another Vigilante Killer case. There weren't that many but it still kept them busy. On top of that, robberies and assaults, muggings and domestic incidents kept being reported with depressing regularity.

Every day, Mike and Adam had a brainstorming session trying to think of other ways to discover the identity of the Vigilante Killer. Yesterday they sat looking at each other and found they had nothing more to add. That day they had tried again and had ended up talking about Gavin and Maria. They needed some type of miracle.

Mike looked at Adam's creation and thought again of Martin Cole and his panic that he was being targeted and would be the next victim of the Vigilante Killer. If he was the next victim, they made sure that there would be no repercussions from their failure to protect him. Mike had spoken to his chief and all their conversations with Martin had been written up word for word. If he was the next to die, what colour would Adam use to write his notes?

Chapter 34

As he left his terraced house wearing his navy blue suit, Martin Cole was too preoccupied with his plans to notice the old lady with the shopping trolley making her way slowly down the road on the opposite pavement. She was just another commuter heading for the train station. The old lady paused, seemingly to rest, and, having noted his house, she moved on.

"It's number one four eight," Dorothea told the others. "I walked up the road and then returned down the alley that runs behind the terrace. Very conveniently, someone has painted the number on the gate which leads from the alleyway to the back of his house."

"Well done, Dorothea. Now we need to monitor his movements for a couple of weeks before we make our final plan." Eve smiled mischievously at her friends.

Amazingly, Martin managed to win a few more times at the bookies and his job was going well. Things were on the up. He barely thought about the Vigilante Killer now but when he did, he laughed at how ridiculously worried he had been. A new job and a new home and he was winning money. At the moment, he felt untouchable. When he got home of an evening and locked the door of his house, he felt completely safe.

Although he was working for someone else, which wasn't ideal, Martin found that he was enjoying himself. He was a born salesman and was making more sales than any of the other staff. He was happy to carry on in this way for a little while. Names of clients were being collected for any future endeavours and he managed to keep some of the money he was earning rather than watching it disappear over the counter at the bookmakers.

The other salesmen and staff at the double glazing firm found themselves wary of Martin. He wasn't rude or aggressive but he never joined in any staff activities and you would never find him engaging in small talk. There was an element of jealousy from them about his success but they all thought there was something else that was off about him.

Martin noticed the sideways glances and the sudden silences when he entered the office. He could almost feel their resentment and suspicion. All his life, he had been aware that people were guarded around him. He, of course, assumed that this was because he was superior to them and, therefore, they felt intimidated by him. It could also be because he was a psychopath.

The ladies had temporarily lost Martin Cole. He left his job at the chicken factory and shortly after, he moved out of the hostel. Martin had been strutting around feeling that destiny was lining up his perfect life for him but Penny had shared in his luck when she saw him leaving the double glazing firm. She hadn't been in disguise, she was just out running an errand, and there he was. He was dressed in a suit and carrying a folder with the firm's logo on it. She reported back to her friends what she had seen and they agreed that he was most likely working for them.

Following him home from work proved problematic because he often visited clients in the evenings. When he had entered the house in Station Road for the third time, they were pretty sure they had found his home. They knew nothing about what he had done to Jimmy since he left prison but they were sure that it would not be long before he set some new nefarious scheme in motion. Their aim was to stop him before his plan came to fruition.

There had been a close call in Martin's first few weeks in his new job. He had been asked to call at the home of a couple to give them a quote. As he arrived at their home, he got a feeling of déjà vu. He had been to this house before. He checked the paper work and read the name and knew why he recognised the house. The occupants had invested money in his Ponzi scheme.

He telephoned one of his colleagues and said that he could not make his appointment due to an emergency. The colleague was astonished that Martin was giving up one of his hot leads but he did not hesitate to step in and set out immediately to see the clients. Along with all his other gifts, Martin had a good memory and he berated himself for not noticing the name of the customers sooner. He would not make that mistake again.

In the evening, Martin would cook simple meals in his small kitchen or get a takeaway pizza, which he had become quite fond of, and then he would watch a soap opera. He was quite fussy about his home which he kept neat and tidy. If there was a speck of dirt on the carpet, he would vacuum and the kitchen surfaces were immaculate. The rest of his evening would be spent reviewing the list of clients he had made and researching various scams on the internet. He couldn't do the Ponzi again so he had been trying to think of a new angle and he had just had a brilliant idea.

Bizarrely, he had been reading an article about the Vigilante Killer and the profiles of his victims. One of them was a builder called John Hall, who had done cheap work for pensioners but charged high prices. He was now thinking of doing something similar but in a more refined way. He would visit his clients, who all trusted him now, and say that he was now representing a building company. If they needed any work, he would produce a quote for an inflated price and employ a builder to do it on the cheap. He could probably find a builder to work with on all his jobs and cut him in on the profit.

He would ring up local builders over the next couple weeks and ask them to call at his house and give him a quote for building work. He could then question them and see if he could find a likeminded individual to join his enterprise. He needed someone much like himself, someone who had no conscience.

A number of builders visited Station Road over the next couple of weeks. Martin could tell who the reputable builders were by asking them about building methods and materials; he had thoroughly researched his subject. A few were legitimate, one of them had a good line in patter so didn't really need a front man. One who turned up was scruffy and didn't smell too pleasant; that wouldn't go down well with his clients and then there was Dean Robertson.

When he came to call, Dean had made an effort to look presentable but it hadn't really worked. He was vague about what was needed to complete the job and quoted a price that was higher than the others. Martin showed the other quotes to Dean.

"All right mate, use someone else then." Dean started to get defensive.

Martin calmed him down. "The figure you came up with is interesting. Do you get many jobs when you are obviously overcharging? I want to know because I think I could help you by being a front man and getting you more work. We could come to an arrangement on how to split the profits. I already have a list of people that may be suitable."

Dean was very interested in Martin's offer. He could see the advantage of having a slick front man like Martin visiting the potential customers. All he would have to do would be complete the work for as low a price as possible. He would not discuss the costs with the client, all negotiations would be done by Martin who would know how far he could push them on price. The excessive profits would then be split between him and Martin.

He wasn't naive. Dean knew that Martin would keep a higher percentage of the profits. He was prepared to go along because it meant that he would have a steady stream of work which would still pay more than average. Martin had been persuasive and Dean agreed to the plan but he did feel wary of him. There was something about his manner, superior and distant, that made him uncomfortable. Martin Cole was not the type of man to be crossed. Martin checked that his front door and back door were locked and then went to bed. He would sleep soundly tonight knowing that his new scheme was under way.

Chapter 35

Dorothea was currently drawing one of her diagrams showing the gate and back yard of Martin's terraced house. It would be far too difficult to enter the property from the front. The road was covered by CCTV as it led from the high street to the town station.

This was the big one, the one that they wanted to get right. They were going to make their plan as foolproof as possible, so that they could complete the task and be free to enjoy their lives afterwards. There would have to be more surveillance to make sure Martin didn't have visitors and to estimate what hours he kept. Eve would have to get into the house as quietly as possible and then deal with the honoured guest, as he had been dubbed.

Dorothea saw builders' vans parked outside Martin's home over the last couple of weeks, but all was quiet again now. He didn't seem to have any friends to call on him and didn't go anywhere at night They had observed the lights in, what they guessed, was the front bedroom going out between eleven o'clock and midnight every night.

The neighbours either side of Martin's house were elderly and the ladies didn't anticipate them being awake in the early hours of the morning. They checked for security lights and there were none covering the back yard. Eve would be able to change into her onesie in the dark back yard before attempting to get into the house. She would strike in the early hours, around two am, on Tuesday morning.

The first obstacle was the gate which had a standard bolt on it. After much discussion, they finally decided to keep it simple. Dorothea would accompany her and give her a leg up over the surrounding six foot wall. On the way out, she could simply undo the bolt. It was unlikely that Eve would find another unlocked door, so she would finally get to use her lock picking skills.

Once in the house, Eve would creep upstairs and stab the heinous Martin Cole where he slept. She had sharpened her knife and practiced her lock picking on the doors of her friends and she was ready to murder him. They had planned as much as they could and now, again, they would hope that good fortune would be on their side.

Eve was wearing the brown wig and the brown anorak on her way to one four eight Station Road. Dorothea was the old lady with trolley. They entered the alley through the back streets avoiding the main road which was covered by CCTV cameras. They moved silently and slowly until they reached the gate with the number painted on it. Thankfully, Eve was small and light, making it easy for Dorothea to boost her up.

She slipped over the wall and waited for her bag of equipment to be passed over.

She was on her own now. It was too dangerous for Dorothea to lurk in the alley at two o'clock in the morning on her own. She set off back to her car. In the darkness of the backyard, Eve produced her lock picks and knife. She put on her gloves, knelt in front of the door, and tried the door knob. As expected, it was locked. A deep breath and she started the process of gaining entry to the property. It took her a few minutes but she kept calm, persevered, and was eventually rewarded with a satisfying click.

She entered the small but neat kitchen and lit her way with a tiny pen torch. It was a risk using a light but less of a risk than banging into something and making a noise. Slow, careful steps, frequent small bursts of light. Progress was cautious. Up the stairs testing each one to ensure there were no loud creaks. At the top, heading for a door which was the entrance to a room at the front of the house. They had not been entirely sure that this would be Martin's bedroom but it seemed the most likely choice.

As she stood at the door, she listened for a moment and all she could hear was a faint snoring. He was in the room and he was asleep. Eve hesitated, not because she was having second thoughts but because she wanted to savour the moment. She opened the door and strode into the room. The time for stealth was over. Get to the side of the bed and finish him off as quickly as possible.

Martin was asleep curled on one side with his back to Eve. She leant over and placed the knife on his neck and slowly increased the pressure. She hoped that he was awake now and aware of what was happening.

"Hello Michael, my honoured guest, my name is Eve Carmichael," she said. "I am your murderer."

Martin didn't gurgle or wheeze or squeal. He rolled onto his back and let out a gasp. Eve would never be certain but she liked to think that he heard what she said and knew who she was.

As she looked down on the dying fraudster, Eve could feel the anger and frustration being stripped away. Seeing Martin Cole breathing his last, lying in a pool of blood, was wonderful. This act, and the other murders, had avenged so many people. Did they all feel this relief when they read of the demise of their persecutors? Knowing that she was responsible for them ending up like that made it even better. She smiled down at Martin, but he was gone. There was a temptation to stab him a couple more times because this murder was personal. That would be a bit of a giveaway so she pulled herself together and thought about getting out of there.

***

In his last seconds, Martin felt the knife go into his neck. He was utterly confused due to being half asleep. Someone was talking to him. Someone was murdering him. He heard the name Eve Carmichael and remembered who she was. He was weak and fading fast but rolled onto his back and gasped a final breath as he saw the hooded figure with goggles and mask, holding a knife dripping with his blood.

***

The deed was done but now she needed to get away. She noted that blood had pooled on the bed. She checked the floor(no blood)and then left knowing that there would be no footprints left behind. Outside, in the back yard, she changed her clothes, unbolted the gate, and made her way back down the alley to the maze of streets that lay beyond. It was a Monday night so there was little chance of running into late night revellers and she was too early for the morning joggers or commuters. No one was seen on her journey back to her house, only a short distance away.

Eve had home town advantage and chose the quietest streets to walk down until she reached her home. Once again, she couldn't use her mobile phone in the middle of the night to inform the others but, in a few hours, she would meet with Penny at Dorothea's and give them the news they longed to hear.

At six thirty, Eve arrived at her friend's and, when she entered the kitchen through the back door, she simply nodded in confirmation that the mission was complete. For a few seconds, they were silent and then, one by one, they began to cry. It was good crying. They were finally able to put the past behind them and move on. Tea was made, tissues were distributed, and the ladies hugged each other.

Eve went off to work after telling her friends about Martin Cole's death and what she had said to him. Penny was working that day too and left ten minutes later. They had been forced to do some serious repairs to their makeup after all the tears but left the house on a high. Dorothea picked up a pad and made a shopping list for the week ahead after she had washed up their tea mugs. They were not having to act in a normal way. For the first time, in many years, they were feeling normal.

Chapter 36

The same night Martin Cole met his demise, Mike Nash and Adam Ashton were following Gavin Vincent to see what he was doing. Mike doubted he would be found to be making components. Adam followed him in his own car from the house and contacted Mike by phone once he had discovered Gavin's final destination. This was the third night in a row that they had watched him.

The first night of their observation revealed Gavin leaving home and going to the cinema and then to a late night cafe. The second night, he went to the pub and then to the cafe. This night was different. He left in work clothes and then went into a public toilet with a bag and exited wearing a suit. He then made his way to a restaurant. Adam went inside ten minutes later and saw him sat with a woman in her forties.

They were smiling and chatting and holding hands.

Adam phoned Mike to say that he was in a restaurant and Gavin was there with a woman. He managed to take a photograph of the couple and then left. Mike was looking at the picture of the smiling couple and shaking his head.

"I knew it. He's up to his old tricks."

Adam tried to be the voice of reason. "We don't know anything for sure."

Mike explained very clearly what he was sure was happening. Why, he asked, was Gavin spending his evenings sat in a late night cafe? Why was he having dinner with another woman? How could he afford to buy Maria a new car if he was not at work making components? The money had to be coming from somewhere. The money was coming from the woman in the photograph and maybe from other women too.

The dilemma for Mike now was what did he do with the information and the photograph? If he spoke to Maria, she may not be grateful to him and she would wonder why he was looking into Gavin's life in the first place.

"What do we do now?" Adam had asked.

"I don't know. I'm going to have to give this some thought." Mike got Adam to send him a copy of the photo and then went home and spent a sleepless night wondering what action to take.

The only thing he could do, Mike decided, was broach the subject with Maria. She would not thank him whichever way he put it. If he had been digging into Gavin's background, that would be wrong. He would say that Adam had gone into a restaurant and thought he saw Gavin but wasn't sure it was him. He could not remember hearing that Gavin and Maria had broken up, so why was he sat there with a different woman. He had taken a photo and shown Mike who was horrified to see that it was Gavin and he was not with Maria.

The timing of the revelation was crucial. He would have to wait until Maria was alone. Adam thought they should keep following Gavin for a couple of weeks to see if there was more than one woman as Mike suspected. Two photos of two different women would be overwhelming proof that Gavin was playing around.

That was settled then. Mike and Adam would continue to watch Gavin and, after a couple of weeks, if their suspicions were confirmed, he would visit Maria and have a very difficult conversation. Gavin and Maria were relegated in the order of priorities when, two days later, they got a call to say another body had been found.

Chapter 37

Martin Cole had been a conscientious worker. He reported to the office and kept his appointments. It had been important for him to create a good impression on the people he later planned to con. When he hadn't turned up for work, his boss tried to phone him with no success. Customers called the office to ask where their representative was when appointments were missed, so when he was a no show again the next day, a colleague called Nick had been sent to his house.

There was no answer when Nick knocked on the door. The curtains were drawn but when he went to the back of the house, the gate was unbolted and the back door unlocked.

"Hello. Hello Martin?" Nick was calling out as he entered the house. The kitchen was tidy as was the lounge. It was no good; he would have to check upstairs. In the second room he tried, he made the discovery.

It was fairly dark in the room but the large dark stain across the bed sheets could only be one thing, blood. Nick had watched enough programmes on television to know about contaminating the crime scene so he backed out of the room and went outside the way he had come in. Reaching for his phone he dialled the emergency services. It wasn't until he spoke to the police that he started to shake and had to sit down on the ground.

Nick was still sat on the ground when the first police car arrived. He confirmed what he had told the dispatcher during his call and one of the policemen entered the building. The other officer could see that Nick was in a state of shock and chatted to him and patted his shoulder. When he could gather his thoughts, Nick suggested that he should call his office. He was advised to call in but just say there had been an incident and that the police were in attendance. As he recovered, Nick wondered what would happen to Martin's clients.

Back at the office, Nick was surrounded by his colleagues eager to know what had happened after his cryptic phone call. He delivered the news that Martin Cole was dead and that it seemed he was the latest victim of the Vigilante Killer. The policeman who had arrived after he called them had been very kind because he was suffering from shock. He explained how his legs had nearly given way under him and he had to sit down.

The staff and boss at the double glazing company looked at each other in bewilderment when Nick related what he had heard about their former colleague Martin. Apparently, he had been a convicted conman who cheated a lot of people out of money with a fake investment scheme. None of them were quite sure how to feel about the death of Martin. He had been a loner and none of them had made a connection with him. They were shocked someone they knew had died but couldn't muster up any feelings of sorrow.

When Mike and Adam arrived at one four eight Station Road, they were pretty sure what they would find. They knew that this was the home of Martin Cole and that he was likely to be the latest victim of the Vigilante Killer. Thank God they had recorded everything when he refused their offer of protection otherwise the police complaints people would be all over them. Scene of crime officers were suited up and inside the house.

"The victim has a single stab wound to the neck," one of them said and their suspicions were confirmed.

Mike and Adam finally entered the small terraced house and had a look around. There was a pile of paperwork neatly stacked on a coffee table which would be collected and examined. It may or may not have a direct bearing on the case but it would surely make interesting reading. The medical officer confirmed what the other officer had said following his preliminary examination. He had been stabbed in the neck.

This time, they knew the victim had been a fraudster because of their prior contact with him. They brought in a new board; they had run out of room on the other one and pinned a picture of Martin Cole to the top. Adam chose a black pen and began making notes about what they knew so far. The scene of crime people had removed a number of items for testing and they hoped that, this time, they would finally get some luck and find that their killer had left a clue.

The details of Martin Cole's arrest for the Ponzi scheme he ran were retrieved and this supplied a list of the people who had been his victims. They would have to talk to all of them, of course, but it was unlikely that the Vigilante Killer was one of them. They were looking for a man. When the story featured on the news, more victims were likely to come out of the woodwork and that meant more names being added to the already long list.

The ladies had cried with relief when their mission was successful but now, watching the evening news a couple of days later, they were in a celebratory mood. The champagne cork popped as the reporter frowned into the camera as he reported another murder had taken place linked to the Vigilante Killer. He talked about how the police had failed to catch the man responsible and Dorothea, Penny, and Eve raised a glass to that piece of information too.

"Do you think we'll be interviewed by the police?" asked Penny.

"Oh definitely. They'll talk to all his victims," Eve said.

"How exciting," said Dorothea as they all took another sip of champagne.

Mike and Adam were working through the list of people conned by Martin Cole. They were mostly older couples, many of them running their own businesses. They collected the names of the male victims and checked their backgrounds in case one of them was responsible.

Mike and Adam had to carry out the investigation the way they would for any murder. They would look at friends and family first and then, if that revealed nothing, the search would be widened. Any of the murders could be a copycat killing. If it was the Vigilante Killer again, their enquiries into Martin's associates would draw a blank but they had to follow procedure. It was difficult to tackle the investigation knowing that their efforts would likely be in vain.

Station Road was covered by CCTV but not the alleyway behind it. A check would be made to see who had been in the area for the previous couple of weeks but, as the name suggested, the train station was at the end of the road so hundreds of people used the route every day. The police were focused on looking for men and barely glanced at any ladies seen in the videos.

The detectives were identifying men found on the CCTV recordings and arranging to interview them. They had not found any local eye witnesses who saw anyone late at night on the day of the murder. The time of death was estimated at between one o'clock and four o'clock so finding someone out and about or looking out of a window at that time was a long shot. The forensics team always took some time to report back to them and they were now calling them every day asking about progress. As time went on, they were pinning all their hopes on the killer having, hopefully, left a clue.

Chapter 38

The reporter intoned, sounding a bit bored, that police found another victim of the Vigilante Killer. His name was Martin Cole and he had been convicted of fraud after running a Ponzi investment scheme. His many clients had seen all their savings disappear and none of it was recoverable because Cole had gambled it all away. Many people had lost their life savings in the scam and one victim of the scheme had taken his own life when his business was ruined.

The newspapers did a thorough character assassination on Martin Cole, which was not that difficult. Jimmy's mother, Jane, contacted one of the papers and told the story of how he had exploited her brain damaged son. The doctor who treated Martin's mother said that he was concerned with how rapidly she had succumbed to her cancer. He often suspected that her end had been hastened by her son.

The people who lost money in the fake investment scheme were tracked down and interviewed. Eve, Penny, and Dorothea declined the offers of money but their stories were still regurgitated for the public. Women whose husbands had died as a result of Martin Cole's actions couldn't be missed out by the press. The more heart-breaking the story, the more the readers seemed to love it.

It was hard to find a piece that condemned the murder of Martin Cole. The broadsheets touched on the lack of results from the ongoing investigation and managed to say that, despite his heinous crimes, he was still a victim. Most of the other papers were more interested in *his* crimes and inferred that anyone who perpetrated this type of fraud was deserving of a visit from the

Vigilante Killer, whose status of hero with the public was growing with each murder.

The one person saddened by Martin's death was Jimmy. He understood that what Martin had done was wrong. His mother explained that he had cheated and stolen and his boss Mr Evans had been very angry and apologised to Jimmy for putting him at risk by employing Martin. His colleagues at work made a fuss of him as if to reassure him that they would not let anything bad happen again.

The thing was, that for all the camaraderie at work, none of his fellow workers had ever taken time to see Jimmy outside of the factory. He knew that his reluctance to go anywhere different made it hard but they didn't even try. Martin had made the effort to call on him every week. He bought him pizza, his favourite, and coke. There were times, when they were playing cards, when they laughed and had fun. Jimmy went home after he heard the news and had pizza and looked at the playing cards they had used. It was a small ceremony of remembrance for his friend Martin.

As Dorothea, Eve, and Penny watched the news report, their phones began to ring. Kirsty got through to Penny first and wept and laughed at the news in an avalanche of emotions. Laura's call was a little more contained as she asked her mother how she felt and then said that, on the whole, she was rather pleased to hear that Martin Cole was dead. Penny agreed and loved hearing the relief in their voices.

Eve heard from a couple of work friends who were eager to gauge her reaction to the news. She told them that she was relieved and felt that her life could start again. A secret inner smile hid the fact that she was pleased she had killed him.

Malcolm phoned his mother and said that he was pleased Martin had died and asked how she felt. Dorothea said that she was comforted that he was not going to be able to hurt people anymore. She decided to call Robert in America. It would be late there but she was sure he wouldn't mind being disturbed to hear this news. He wasn't disturbed; he was delighted. Robert shed a few tears on the phone to his mother and promised that he would raise a glass the following evening to the Vigilante Killer.

The next day, Robert and Malcolm talked on the phone. Robert was still slightly shell shocked by the news.

"All the times we discussed how we would like to kill him and someone else has done it for us. I'm kind of glad because I don't think I would have had the stomach for it."

Malcolm laughed. "Me neither. This Vigilante Killer is amazing. He kills the bad guys and he gets away with it. I know we shouldn't condone this but, what the hell, I'm a fan."

Chapter 39

The first hours and days after a murder were crucial in that evidence could be lost if not collected or the killer could slip away, maybe even abroad. Details were still fresh in the minds of any eyewitnesses so they needed to talk to them as soon as possible. As the interviews continued, they were left with just women and elderly men to talk to. Not the type of person they were looking for. It was at this stage that Mike decided to take a look through the paperwork found at Martin Cole's house.

The reason Martin had gotten away with his swindle for so long was that he was an intelligent and organised man. The paperwork they collected comprised of a series of files, each of which was labelled. The first one was marked Clients, the next was marked Builders, and the third was marked Pricing. He had used different coloured pens, reminding Mike of the many hued boards in the office that Adam had created.

Mike opened the file labelled Clients and started to read. There was a list of names and beside each one was a date showing when he had visited them and the amount they had spent on windows. There were more columns to show what type of property they owned and then some kind of rating. What did the number mean? Knowing Martin, it probably indicated the level of gullibility.

The file marked builders was the next on the pile. Inside were a number of quotes received from local builders for work to be done on one four eight Station Road. The property was rented, so it was unlikely that Martin was going to have any work done and pay for it himself so why all the quotes? On the back of the letters, there were notes. One builder had been deemed "Too professional," another had been judged on appearance "Scruffy and badly spoken, would not inspire confidence." Included in the file was a quote from Dean Robertson. His was annotated with "already dodgy: approach with idea". This was getting interesting.

He got to the last file which was headed Pricing. Inside this folder were tables which featured a list of jobs such as chimney breast removal, small conservatory, large conservatory, and single storey extension. Next to the jobs were columns showing different prices. The costs in column one, were the cheapest, but still pretty steep by Mike's reckoning, and increased with each column up to number five. The clients from the first file had a rating of one to five.

So, his guess about a gullibility rating looked spot on. It seemed that Martin was indeed setting up another business, fleecing the trusting clients he had befriended. He was intending to offer building services to people satisfied with their double glazing but, this time, overcharge them for shoddy work. The more trusting and wealthy they were, the higher the price would be. This also gave them a new, but unlikely, suspect. Dean Robertson.

Adam and Mike were very interested to talk to their new suspect. Dean was a bad builder who was not averse to overcharging his customers. Having a respectable front man like Martin Cole could have helped him earn a lot more money but what if Martin had decided against using Dean? Had Dean tried to take out the competition by getting rid of him? There had been one copycat killer, could this be another.

When the police contacted him again, Dean was worried. He had seen on the news that Martin Cole had been killed and he was hoping that the quote he had sent would not seem relevant. But the call had come. He was nervous about what the police had found. He would be seeing Detective Inspector Nash and his sidekick again. They were the ones that had upset him last time. All that talk of the Vigilante Killer had panicked him badly. He'd even bought a bloody dog.

As he sat waiting in an interview room, all kinds of things were going through Dean's mind. Being a murder suspect hadn't even occurred to him. When Detective Inspector Nash came in holding some files, he was only worried about the latest job he had botched. Adam followed Mike into the room and they went through the formalities before the first folder was opened.

"You have heard about the death of Martin Cole? When we searched his house, we found some very interesting files. It seems he was planning a new business. We think you may know something about it."

Dean shifted uncomfortably in his seat. He had sent a quote so they must know that they had met. The plan had never progressed because Martin died so they couldn't charge him for an idea, could they? He decided that the best thing at this stage was to come clean about what Martin had proposed and get this over and done with.

"It was his idea. He wanted to cheat some people he had done windows for and he tried to get me involved. I never done any work for him."

Mike produced his winning smile. "He got murdered before you could get going, that was a shame. Or was that what you wanted? Take out the middle man and keep all the profits."

Dean's mouth formed a perfect O as he realised why he was being questioned. He wasn't suspected of fraud; he was suspected of murder. "I think I'll have a solicitor now."

The interview was put on hold whilst a duty solicitor was summoned. Dean's reaction had been telling though. It was a nice theory but it didn't look as if it would pan out. Dean was fully focused on the dodgy building scam and utterly shocked when suggested that he had played a part in Martin's demise.

Another interview had led to another dead end. The chance of Dean being the murderer was slim at best, they had known that when they went into the interrogation. The killer in this case had been clever and controlled and careful. These were not traits that one would attribute to Dean Robertson. Just like the previous murders, there appeared to be no clues left behind.

An hour and a half later, Dean was released by the police and made his way home. He was angry with Martin Cole. He was dragged to the station because the stupid bugger had left notes about their new business and that annoyed him. The fact that Martin had been killed before they had a chance to make any money annoyed him even more.

As he walked up the front path of his house, the dog began to bark. “Shut up Prince, it’s me.” The dog carried on barking.

Chapter 40

Although he was in the middle of the latest murder case, Mike was still preoccupied by the situation regarding Maria and Gavin. He and Adam had not had the time to follow him again but he had the photograph and could not procrastinate about its use for much longer. If he got out of the office at a reasonable time one evening, he would go to his ex-wife's house and give her the bad news.

***

Gavin was a charmer from the time he was a small child. He had blonde curls and had discovered early that smiles and persuasion worked much better than tantrums and tears. As he entered his teenage years, he became popular with girls and there were some who would do anything to attract, and then keep, his attention. At first, he was content with just receiving sexual favours but, when his dates offered to pay for things, he saw another opportunity.

He was bright academically but found school boring. He knew he was clever and attractive and he had already determined that he would be making his way in life using those characteristics rather than applying himself through hard work. When things came easily to you, it was hard to keep your feet on the ground. Gavin began at an early age to grow a sense of entitlement and an inflated ego. He liked to be adored by the women he conned and couldn't conceive any of them falling out of love with him.

Unlike Simon Butler, Gavin liked most of the women he had conned. Not that he would ever have used the word conned. He liked nice things and he had persuaded his lady friends to pay for them. If they handed him cash as well, that was a nice bonus. There had been a complaint from one disgruntled ex to the police, which had been a close shave, but he got away with it. He charmed his girlfriends and took what was offered but he had never been too greedy.

When Gavin met Maria, he fell in love. The other women he was stringing along were quickly disposed of and he was even prepared to put up with her child, Phoebe. Usually, his girlfriends were older ladies with no children or grown up children. He had always worked but had never had a good job or been promoted because he got bored easily and would move on. Now he had to earn some decent money so he could look after Maria and make her happy. Maria's ex-husband was a police detective, another incentive to make money the regular way.

It was hard going to a job he didn't like day after day. How did people do this and not go out of their minds, thought Gavin. The half decent job that he had secured still didn't seem to pay enough to meet all the bills that he and Maria received, even with the money she got from her ex-husband to pay for the kid. For a while he had tried his best, even working overtime when it was offered, but lately he was tired of making an effort.

At least once a week, Gavin phoned in sick or came late. The inevitable happened and he was called into the boss's office and given a warning. He tried to do better for a couple of weeks before the bad habits returned and he was fired. Gavin kept a secret savings account where he had some of the proceeds from his generous girlfriends. He had not wanted to tell Maria that he lost his job so he dipped into this to contribute to the bills and the lack of money provoked a series of rows with Maria.

Desperate times called for desperate measures. Gavin adored Maria and the only way he could keep her happy was to make enough income to pay the bills and buy her treats Gavin had rapidly got rid of his girlfriends, when he met Maria. He disappeared from their lives without a word. He now made a series of phone calls to the women and gave excuses for his departure.

"I'm so sorry I haven't been in contact. I have been working abroad as a consultant. I can't talk too much about it if you know what I mean, secret stuff. God, I've missed you. I couldn't tell you what was going on but I'm back now. If you can find it in your heart to forgive me, maybe we can see each other again. It's been hell."

He was broken hearted he had to leave without letting them know what was happening, he said. How could they even think that he didn't love them anymore?

There were tears and accusations but, one by one, the women chose to believe his fantastical story and allowed him back into their lives. He was still very busy with his work, he told them, so he could not see them as much as he would like. He arranged a few dates and mentioned the difficulty of transferring money from the Middle East, where he had been working. It didn't take long for the first offer of monetary assistance to arrive.

One of the ladies was particularly smitten by Gavin and, when he talked about his lack of transport, she gave him her old car. What was old to her was barely used to most people. Gavin gave the five-year-old vehicle as to Maria. What with all the other things he was able to buy for the house, he was now firmly in her good books after the slight hiccup when he had been short of funds.

Maria loved the car he had given her, and they were now blissfully happy again. He would have to start watching his weight. The dining out with his lady friends and the lovely Italian meals Maria made for him were having a disastrous effect on his waistline. The downside of his double life was the nights when he didn't have a date and had to go out anyway. He couldn't be making that much money only working two or three nights a week so for the sake of appearances, he went out and visited the pub or a cafe the rest of the time.

There were times when Gavin shuddered at the thought of what would happen if he was found out. He had never particularly worried about the consequences of his actions but much more was at stake now, his beautiful Maria. Gavin never pushed the women he had taken money from too hard but now he used sob stories and cried and pouted to get more and more out of them. He was playing a dangerous game.

***

As Mike left work at eight o'clock after another frustrating day, he could put it off no longer. He looked at the photograph stored on his phone and headed for his car. This was the day. The day when he would tell Maria that Gavin had been cheating on her and very likely using money he had conned from women to pay for all her new things.

Maria opened the door when Mike knocked and stood squarely in the door frame. “Why are you here? Is there a problem about taking Phoebe this weekend?”

“No, it’s not that. Is Gavin at home?”

Maria confirmed that he was at work and Mike said that in that case could he come in because he needed to talk to her about something. She grudgingly let him in but didn’t look too pleased about it.

Chapter 41

“I need to talk to you about something I found out about Gavin.”

The words were barely out of Mike’s mouth and Maria was on her feet. Phoebe was in bed so Maria didn’t shout; it was more of a fierce whisper.

“I knew it. You couldn’t help yourself, could you? You had to stick your policeman’s nose into my business.”

When Maria finally stopped her rant, Mike carried on. He explained that Adam had seen someone who he thought was Gavin in a restaurant. He took a photograph of him and sent it to Mike. At this point, Mike produced his phone, found the picture, and showed it to Maria. The image, at a slightly odd angle, featured Gavin smiling at a woman with whom he was holding hands.

Mike then told Maria what he had found out about Gavin's past. There was a complaint against him from a woman about borrowing large sums of money and not paying it back. When questioned, Mike had to admit that the case hadn't gone to court but he trotted out the cliché of there being no smoke without fire. He knew from the look on his wife's face that she was not convinced.

Maria sat down again. "How happy this must make you. Not content with breaking my heart when you moved out, you now come up with this. As a detective, you should know that a picture doesn't prove a thing. It could have been taken at any time. It could be a picture of him with a family member or an old friend. And the complaint from a scorned woman that didn't even go to court is hardly conclusive."

Mike was going to use the word denial when he realised what his ex-wife had said.

"Hang on a minute. I broke your heart when I moved out. You asked me to leave!"

Maria gave an exasperated sigh and explained to Mike that she had hoped that asking him to leave would bring him to his senses and make him spend more time at home. Mike then explained that he left because she had asked but never really wanted to go. He thought he was doing the right thing by giving her some space.

The two of them sat in silence as they contemplated this conversation. Mike ruined the moment when he said that her moving Gavin into their home so quickly had been the final straw. Maria turned slowly to look at him and he knew another eruption was about to happen.

"So it was my fault. And now you are taking revenge by trying to ruin my relationship with Gavin or should I refer to him as the final straw."

The conversation, or argument, that ensued went around and around. Mike tried to convince Maria that his intentions were altruistic but she was having none of it. She was not listening to reason. She had made up her mind about why Mike was there and it had nothing to do with having her best interests at heart. Gavin was a good man who would not behave like that. He was attentive and caring and generous. Mike pointed out that he was being generous with someone else's money but this only caused a momentary pause in Maria's list of Gavin's attributes.

As Mike listened, he became resigned to the fact that whatever he said would be explained away by Maria. He was the enemy now, the bad guy trying to make her unhappy again. What he had heard during this evening made him think though. Maria asked him to leave but had not really wanted him to go. Before he left the house, he told Maria how he felt and then, if she finally came to her senses, there may be a chance of reconciliation.

The tirade was winding up. Maria had run out of things to say and was glaring at him and asking him to leave. It was now or never.

"I've never wanted you to be unhappy. Everything I have done is because I love you. I left because you asked me to but I thought that we would get back together. I hoped and prayed that we would get back together. When you moved Gavin into our home, my heart was broken. I'm here today because I still care for you and I don't want you to get hurt by Gavin who is, whether you choose to believe it or not, a bad man. I'm going now. If you need me, give me a call."

Mike stood up and made his exit on slightly wobbly legs. He was not used to baring his soul and he was finding it very hard to make a dignified exit after his speech. Maria was still sat on her new sofa as she heard the door shut behind Mike. What a terrible mess they had made of their marriage, both of them too stubborn to say what they were really thinking. She realised that tears were running down her face.

She also had to think about the picture she had seen of Gavin and the things that Mike had said. His sudden change to working at night and the amount of money he was earning had been a surprise. She should have asked more questions when he presented her with a new car. Maria put her head in her hands as the suspicion caught hold. She had been naive.

Even with the dawning realisation that Mike could be right, Maria couldn't bring herself to give up yet. She would ask Gavin some subtle questions and see if there were reasonable explanations for the dramatic change in their circumstances. If she wasn't happy with what he said, she would have to talk to Mike.

"How's your job going?" Maria asked Gavin on a Sunday morning.

He announced that he would have to work Saturday nights sometimes and hoped she didn't mind. Working at the weekend would mean extra money. Gavin said that he was working hard but that he didn't mind if it made their life better. When Maria suggested that she would rather have him home more than have extra money, he became a bit defensive.

"I'm doing this for us," he pouted. "I thought you would be grateful."

The next question from Maria, which was about what Gavin actually did, at the business whose name she didn't know, made him extremely uncomfortable. He muttered something about components and, when pressed, he said it was far too technical for her to understand. Maria backed off at this stage because she wasn't entirely sure how Gavin would react if she pushed him further. That thought alone was troubling and she knew that something had to be done.

The next day Maria phoned Mike. When he answered the call, all she could do was cry. When she caught her breath, she said, "I don't know what to do. Can you help me?"

Mike said that he would take care of things. It may take a little while but he would set up an official enquiry into Gavin and if, as he suspected, he was conning women, he would be arrested. He was getting to play the role of knight in shining armour and he hoped that this would help him win back his lady.

Chapter 42

Adam was looking at Mike as he finished his call with Maria. “Let’s put that scumbag Gavin behind bars,” Mike said and Adam smiled.

He had been waiting for the opportunity to help his boss with this problem. They started to hatch a plan to get Gavin arrested and therefore out of Maria’s life. They had found out enough to warrant taking it further and now that they had the go ahead from Maria, they went into action.

It was time to make it an official enquiry. Mike went to the chief and told him the situation and his suspicions and also the plan to catch Gavin. He fought to be involved in the investigation but was not surprised when he was sidelined because of his personal involvement. He had already overstepped the line by searching the database for details on Gavin. The fraud department would be assigned the case but he would be given a chance to talk to them before he had to stand back and let them do their job.

His colleagues in fraud were only too happy to help. They would observe Gavin and establish who he was seeing. Once they identified the women, they would approach them, reveal the truth about Gavin Vincent, and persuade them to press charges. He wasn't allowed to take part in the operation, but Mike would be kept informed of progress.

It didn't take long to identify three women regularly seen with Gavin. The police contacted them and arranged for them to visit the station at the same time. The women would be confronted with the unpalatable truth about Gavin and would be more disposed, hopefully, to press charges. On the day of the interviews, Mike couldn't help walking through the fraud offices to see the three women sitting in a waiting area eying each other nervously. Later in the day, he heard about the dramatic scenes, shouting, crying, and cursing, after they were told what had been happening. They all wanted to press charges.

The three women were taken into an interview room together and the fraud squad officer opened proceedings by asking them if they knew a Gavin Vincent. He flashed a photograph of the smiling Gavin and Maria at them and then waited for the fall out. He was asked who the woman was and he replied she was the girlfriend that Gavin lived with.

What followed was pandemonium. The detective sat back and let them discuss the betrayal between themselves. They compared the stories they had been told and then admitted to lending him money. The sums being mentioned were significant amounts. One woman had even given him a car.

In each case, he had asked to borrow money. None of the women had, they confessed, expected him to pay all of it back. The fact that it had not been gifted to him meant they could press charges if they so wished. All the women were very keen to press charges. Had they been interviewed separately, they may have decided to sweep it under the carpet but together they had the strength to make a formal complaint.

"The one who gave him the car was hysterical when we told her he had passed it on to his live-in girlfriend. I thought there might be a cat fight, but they bonded in their desire to wreak revenge on Gavin Vincent. Hell hath no fury and all of that. We're going to pick him up at his home tomorrow morning." The fraud officer was telling Mike about the interviews.

Mike then sent Maria a text saying, "All sorted."

Gavin had been out all night and was not best pleased to hear the doorbell ringing over and over again. Whoever it was could sod off; he wasn't getting up. The next sound he heard was a large crash as the police broke open the door. He was stood by the bed in pyjama bottoms when three officers entered the room. He was told that he was being arrested and was read his rights.

At least they let Gavin get dressed but he wasn't allowed to have a shower and wash his hair. He was very fussy about his appearance and didn't want to leave the house without preparing himself. He was dragged out by the police officers and bundled into the back of the car ready for his trip to the station.

At the custody desk, he used his one phone call to contact Maria who simply said that she would pack up his stuff and leave it for him in the garage. She did not want to set eyes on him again. She did not sound surprised and she didn't ask him for any details. Gavin wondered if Maria's ex-husband Mike had been instrumental in his arrest. The more he thought about it, the more certain he was that the damn detective was the cause of his downfall.

Maria was very thorough as she made sure every item that was Gavin's was packed up and put in the garage. She did not want him to have an excuse to get back into her home. How would he behave towards her when he realised that she had played a part in his downfall? His actions were not those of someone in their right mind and who knew what threat he could pose to her and Phoebe.

When Gavin was released on bail, he headed for Maria's house. He banged on the now repaired front door. He tried the back door. He shouted through the letter box. He cried and begged but it made no difference. He persevered for a couple of hours but had to concede defeat in the end. The garage door opened, he found his possessions in a couple of suitcases and some boxes. He took his stuff and left, but he would come back again. Maria was the love of his life and he wasn't going to give up the fight for her. That night, in a bed and breakfast's shabby room, he cried himself to sleep. Why was life so unfair?

The next day, Gavin showered and shaved and dressed carefully. He stopped at a florist and bought some roses and then went to Maria's home. After two more hours of begging and pleading, he left. He knew she was in there; he had seen her through the window but she was unmoved by his pleas. Gavin would change tactics and catch her out in the open. He would be at the school gates when Phoebe came out of school.

Chapter 43

Following the death of Martin Cole, the ladies were in reflective mood. The tears provided an emotional release and the euphoria that followed was the feeling of freedom from the past that they all felt. Now that their nemesis was dead, their lust for revenge had been fully sated.

Dorothea looked at her dear friends and said what they were all thinking. “I think we’re done.” They agreed wholeheartedly and the mood around the table lightened now that the decision was made. Life would now go back to normal, whatever that meant, and they were pleased if a little adrift.

The ladies arranged to go to the lock up garage the following Wednesday and have a bonfire. They had purchased a galvanised incinerator bin which they kept in the garage, ready for the day when they had to dismantle the operation. They arrived and set up the incinerator on nearby wasteland and then returned to the garage. They picked up the boxes containing the wigs, clothes, coveralls, and the knife and then set off in a solemn procession towards the burner.

As each item was placed into the bin, they reflected, and sometimes commented, on the role it had played in the murders. They were delighted to see the back of the ugly brown anorak but some of the wigs were like old friends. The coveralls emitted a foul stench as their manmade fibres caught fire. They had been bizarre but vital and had given their guests a moment of sublime bewilderment as they breathed their last.

The red hoodie went in and the trainers that Penny and Eve had worn. The magazine that gave them the details of John Hall and all the notes were added. The computer and the knife went in but they were doubtful that the fire would have the capability of destroying all trace of them.

More fuel was added from time to time to ensure that the inferno continued until everything was gone.

The whole event had a ritual like quality as they loaded the contents of the boxes carefully into the bin. A liberal dose of lighting fluid was added and a match struck. Dorothea, Eve, and Penny joined hands as they watched the tools of their murderous trade consumed by the flames.

After the fire died down, they raked through the ashes to make sure nothing was left. Part of the knife remained and this was carefully removed with a gloved hand and would be discarded later. The tablet computer was a solid lump of plastic but they had another go at burning it to ensure it was truly dead. Still not happy, they smashed it with a hammer and then put what was left into some drain cleaner which contained sulphuric acid.

Anything left over was carefully collected and taken away. Over the next couple of days, Penny picked a couple of takeaway cartons out of bushes and placed the leftover parts of the computer and knife inside. The cartons were then disposed of in waste paper bins in the town centre. They would disappear into landfill never to be seen again.

The newspapers were full of the details, both real and imagined, of the Martin Cole murder, the fourth by the Vigilante Killer. As former victims of his con, each of the ladies were contacted again and asked to rehash their stories or give quotes. They all said something along the lines of how they had put the past behind them but were not surprised that someone had taken the law into their own hands. They didn't want to be featured in articles but supplied the simple quote.

A period of calm descended over the friends.. They still met every Sunday but now new topics of conversation crept in. Before Martin's death, they talked about cookery and sadness and loss. Now they talked about cookery and the future.

Their mood was fatalistic as far as the murders and getting caught were concerned. As time passed, they began to believe they had got away with it. There were more hurdles to jump before they could relax completely but for the moment things were looking pretty good. They did occasionally talk about their work but it was usually a passing reference in connection with a news item.

The papers and television news were full of the latest killing. Hearing about the murders took on a slightly surreal quality for the friends. It was the culmination of their vendetta and, had it not been reported on so frequently, they may have not believed that it had finally happened. The pictures of the four victims were usually shown together. This rogue's gallery of victims evoked no sympathy when viewed by the public.

When the ladies subsequently read the stories about what Martin had done to the poor man Jimmy, who was brain damaged, and what he might have done to his own mother, they were pleased they had seized the opportunity to finish him off. Details of what Martin Cole was planning for the future with his building scam were also reported. There was not a single redeeming feature unearthed about him.

Dorothea and Penny had worried about how Eve would cope. She was the one who carried out the murders and they were concerned that she would suffer some trauma as a result. It wasn't as if she could go and get therapy if she needed it. They offered their help if it was needed but Eve assured them that she was glad it was all over. If she had to do it all again, she would.

Penny saw the murder of John Hall but viewed it dispassionately and assured her friends that she was not unduly troubled by the memory. Dorothea did not regret her part in the killings but admitted she had become quite fond of the grey wig and tartan shopping trolley disguise and would miss them. The trolley had been left outside a charity shop as a donation and was now probably owned by a naturally silver haired person.

On the day that she got a call saying that the police wanted to interview her and that it was just as a matter of routine, Dorothea phoned her friends and warned them that it was likely they would receive calls too. They received the calls and found themselves reporting to the station for interview. They were tense but the only way to deal with this was to meet it head on and face whatever was thrown at them.

Chapter 44

Mike and Adam were working their way through the interviews with the victims of Martin Cole's Ponzi scheme. None of the people they had spoken to were that sorry to hear of his death although some spoke about how charming and trustworthy he had seemed when he persuaded them to part with their money.

The men had been their main focus but they did not feel the investigation was done thoroughly unless they talked to everyone involved. The three star witnesses at Martin's trial were some of the last to be questioned. They had suffered more than most, losing their husbands, but they were unlikely suspects.

Dorothea, the oldest of the three, had a stately demeanour. She was tall but stood upright and spoke in an even tone with just a hint of her Caribbean roots discernible in her accent. Mike asked her if she had read about Martin Cole's death.

"Oh yes. I've been following it on the television news as well. You read about murder but you never think that it will feature someone you know." She was asked how she felt about it. "Honestly, I would have to say I was quite pleased. He didn't kill my husband Royston; he died of cancer but the stress he caused contributed to his death I'm sure."

She was questioned about her whereabouts on the night of the murder. She could tell that the policeman's heart wasn't really in the interview but he had to go through his list of questions so that he could tick some boxes, she supposed. The good looking detective and his boyish assistant were very kind, one of them brought her a cup of tea, and she left after twenty minutes of the nicest interrogation imaginable.

Eve was the next to attend an interview. She was asked how she felt about Martin Cole's demise and she smiled at the handsome detective who she had seen on television. She was delighted, she said. That man had stolen their money and caused her husband to have a heart attack. At this point, she paused and wiped away a tear before putting a grimly determined smile back onto her face.

The box ticking questions were asked and Eve bravely carried on with the process after taking a sip of water. Mike admired this woman who had been through so much. She was tiny in stature but stood six feet tall in his eyes. To dust herself off and keep going after such losses was incredible. When she left, Mike wished her the best for the future.

"You know, I think his death has put a line under the whole thing. I'm ready to move on now," she said.

Penny went into her interview having spoken to her friends first. She was relaxed when the detectives questioned her knowing they weren't under suspicion. She played her slightly ditzy grandmother role to perfection. Her response to the question about Martin's death was to shyly admit that she had been happy. She said that she had phoned her friends Eve and Dorothea and they were relieved he wouldn't cheat anyone else. She even inquired if the detectives had spoken to the other ladies.

When they asked her for an alibi, Penny began to go back day by day over the last few weeks in an effort to remember where she had been. In the end, Mike told her not to worry about it. He had read about her husband's suicide and he hadn't relished bringing it all up again and distressing her. He was more relieved when the interview was over than she was.

As the day ended, Mike and Adam reviewed the interviews they completed that day. Nothing new had been revealed and none of the interviewees were likely suspects. The forensic tests were not giving them any clues. The Vigilante Killer had been as meticulous as ever and had not left DNA or fingerprints or footprints.

Many hours had been spent looking at CCTV pictures of the area and the few cars seen that late at night had been traced and their owners excluded from suspicion. Station road had been deserted for most of the night but, again, those found on CCTV had legitimate reason for being there and were not involved in the murder. They were looking for a car when the murderer had simply walked there and then walked back home.

Adam wrote some notes on the board with his black marker pen. The four faces of the victims looked back at him. He turned to Mike and shrugged. Mike said the words he was hoping to hear "Let's call it a day." They were out of the station within a couple of minutes. Adam had a girlfriend who he was meeting later and Mike was going to see Maria.

The newspapers were still giving the police a hard time about the lack of results in the Vigilante Killer case. The chief knew they had been diligent and relentless in their pursuit of the killer and, even though he was feeling the pressure, he backed his officers when he spoke to the press. They put out numerous appeals for information and a crime programme had focused on the killings but nothing new had emerged.

Chapter 45

The television station and the police liaised on a programme which encouraged the public to help crack unsolved crimes. The Vigilante Killer murders were the perfect subject for the show. Four killings made it sensational enough to provoke interest and, when the production team saw the handsome Detective who was in charge of the case, they knew they were onto a ratings winner.

It was a welcome distraction for Mike from the relentless disappointment of the case and the problems with Gavin Vincent. Sometimes the programme showed reconstructions of the crimes but this was not appropriate for this case. The format would be different this time because they had nothing to reconstruct. Simon, John, and Martin had all been murdered in their own homes and Eddie had left the pub late at night and been murdered on a deserted dark path.

The presenter, Carrie Walters, was going to interview Mike and he could then talk about the dates and times of the murders and appeal for anyone that may have been in the areas at the time to come forward. There were some grainy pictures of potential witnesses, which they would display, in an effort to get them to contact the police.

Mike found himself in a chair having his makeup done, ready for the recording of the show. If they could see him now, Adam and his other colleagues would find it highly amusing and never let him hear the end of it. Carrie stuck her head around the door and asked him how he was. She was going to run through the questions with him and he could practice his answers. She smiled a lot and touched his shoulder as she spoke to him. Another fan of the handsome detective, it would seem.

There was a legal adviser present to ensure that neither Mike nor the presenter said the wrong thing. As filming started, Mike hoped this would lead to the breakthrough they so desperately needed. Carrie did her piece to camera and then turned and introduced Detective Inspector Mike Nash. He was a natural as he answered Carrie's questions clearly and turned to the camera at the appropriate times to speak directly to the audience. He paused when the photographs were displayed and stared intently with his blue eyes into the lens as he pleaded with the public to dig deep into their memories and to get in touch if they remembered anything, however small it may be, that could help them catch the Vigilante Killer.

The estimated times of the murders were given together with the locations and the likely routes that the killer would have taken. The details appeared in a rolling text across the bottom of the screen to ensure that the audience saw the information. Phone numbers for the police were given out and internet addresses were supplied so that they knew they had covered every possible means of communication.

Carrie leaned forward and took Mike's hand and thanked him for appearing on the show. She was rewarded by one of his smiles and she smiled back. For a moment, she had quite forgotten herself. She tore her eyes away and looked back at the camera and wrapped up that segment of the show. He had barely left his seat when the producer was approaching him to see if he wanted a regular spot on the programme.

Eve, Dorothea, and Penny were watching the show together. It had been extensively advertised and they were keen to see what they had to say.

"Oh, good, it's the handsome detective." Eve looked at her friends who nodded approvingly.

He was introduced by Carrie Walters and launched into his appeal. At one point, a blurry photograph appeared on screen of a youth on a scooter.

"It's you, Eve!" Penny was very excited to see her on television.

They paused the action and studied the picture. Eve's head was down so you couldn't see her face and the beanie hat covered her hair. There was no way you could identify her from the photo, they determined. The interview continued and they watched Carrie as she smiled at the detective and held his hand as he finished.

"Look, she's flirting with him. You can't blame her though," said Dorothea.

Later in the programme, Carrie gave an update of the information that had been received by them so far. She talked about calls naming possible killers and reports of a man seen near John Hall's home. She tried to make it sound like they had made a major breakthrough but the response to the appeal had been somewhat underwhelming. The ladies chuckled at the lack of witnesses which they were very pleased about.

As time passed, it became less and less likely they would find the culprit. Once again, they would have to wait for another murder and hope that the killer made a mistake. Four unsolved murders were hanging over the force but they were at a dead end. Mike was distracted at the moment and not particularly worried about his arrest record. Gavin was out of Maria's house but he was not yet out of her life.

Chapter 46

When Mike arrived at his ex-wife's house, she opened the door and ushered him in quickly. As she did this, she scanned the view up and down the street and relaxed when she didn't catch sight of Gavin.

"Have you seen him today?" Mike asked.

"No, just a few phone calls which I haven't answered. I think the police you sent did the trick."

Since he had been ejected from the house, Gavin had been trying desperately to get back in. He was still madly in love with Maria and was convinced that if he could talk to her, he would be able to persuade her to take him back. For several days after his release on bail, he had spent hours outside her house and had waited outside

Phoebe's school in the hope of snatching a few words with Maria when she went to pick her up.

After he had appeared at the school, the Headmistress was informed that he was not to go anywhere near Phoebe and he wasn't to be admitted onto school property. One of Maria's friends was allowed to drive in through the gates, where she picked up her child and Phoebe, and then delivered her home. As she passed Gavin in the car, Phoebe looked out of the back window and stuck her tongue out at him. He had been thwarted in his attempts to speak to Maria thus far but he wasn't giving up.

Maria was beginning to feel like a prisoner in her own house. Mike arranged for a police car to cruise by the house on a regular basis and this had deterred Gavin from his vigil. He still phoned her mobile several times a day, leaving tearful pleading messages. Long texts with declarations of his love also pinged into the phone all the time.

Maria was making arrangements to change her phone but she wasn't sure that he would be put off by having that source of access curtailed.

Unfortunately, Maria had been correct. Gavin changed tactics and wrote letters and sent cards adorned with hearts and kittens and all things twee. Maria didn't like twee. She hadn't responded to any of his contacts and could now only hope that he would give up his futile quest. Mike had got Gavin out of her house and was now doing all he could to prevent him bothering her further.

Mike was somewhat conflicted about the situation with Gavin. He was gone from the house but was now stalking Maria obsessively, troubling to say the least. Maria's fear had meant, however, that Mike was called upon to give assistance and comfort. He had now stayed over at the house several times in his role as protector. After a couple of nights on the sofa, he was now welcomed back into Maria's bed.

Phoebe was a happy child. She loved having her daddy around and her mummy seemed happy now too. She had been questioned closely by her parents when she said that she was glad Gavin had gone. They were worried that something sinister had happened but Phoebe didn't like Gavin because he more or less ignored her. He only made an effort with her when Maria was around to see. When she had tried to talk to him, Gavin's response, on most occasions, had been "Yeah, whatever kid."

***

He stared at his phone as if willing it to ring but, so far, Maria had not returned any of Gavin's calls. That ex-husband had his feet firmly back under the table. Maria needed someone to look after her and as soon as Gavin had gone, he had seized his chance to ingratiate himself with her. Gavin was getting desperate. Before now, Gavin had only ever loved Gavin. Now he loved Maria and he was not going to give up until he got her back.

He had never known such pain as was caused by the absence of the woman he loved. He became angrier and angrier as he imagined her at home with her ex-husband and what they might be doing. The next day, when he made his first call, he was greeted by the message that the number was unavailable. She had changed her phone. Gavin sat on the bed in the small room he rented and sobbed. Once he got himself back under control, he resolved to contact her some other way.

It seemed hopelessly old fashioned but somehow romantic to be outing his feelings in a letter. He wrote about his love for her and reminded her of the happy times they had spent together. He raved about her beauty and her kindness and how she was his soul mate. He signed the letter with a flourish and then thought that he had better mention the kid. He added a PS hoping that Phoebe was well.

The first letter was the only one that Maria read. It was pitiful and embarrassing to look at. When she saw the post script, Maria screwed the letter into a ball and threw it into the bin. Mike watched her and then fished it out again.

"What are you doing? It's evidence," he said. "If you get anymore give them to me."

Letters and cards came thick and fast. Maria handed them unopened to Mike and he put them in a file. When he had the chance, he opened them and read them. He did this partly out of curiosity but also because they might reveal a change in Gavin's mood. One of the letters he read stated that the problems between them would be solved if Mike was out of the way. She could choose to end it with him and send him packing or Gavin would take the matter into his own hands. If she did not reply, he would take this as a sign that he was to proceed with his plan to remove Mike from their lives. This letter was not added to the ones in the file. It was burnt.

There had been a lot of tears over the last few weeks. Not for the loss of the man but because Maria had let Gavin into their lives. She was full of guilt that she had not noticed his indifference to Phoebe and was so grateful that Mike, despite everything that had gone before, came to her rescue. The conversation that Maria and Mike had on the evening that she learned the truth about Gavin Vincent had been a surprise. Why had they split up when it wasn't what either of them had wanted? If she had not met Gavin, maybe they would have gotten back together much sooner. She let Gavin move in because she knew it would hurt Mike and the whole thing backfired spectacularly.

As Mike and Maria discussed the events that led them to this point, they vowed to talk more in the future. They were starting again and they wanted to make sure that they didn't make the same mistakes as before. Life would not be normal for them, however, until Gavin was dissuaded from his present course. He would hopefully end up in prison but, for the time being, he was a problem.

The fear that haunted Mike was what would happen once Gavin stopped pursuing Maria. Would he become superfluous to requirements if she no longer needed his protection? He hoped this would not end the rekindling of the relationship but the only way to find out was to stop Gavin harassing Maria. He would have to seriously think about how this could be achieved.

Mike kicked off his shoes and ditched his tie and jacket as he settled onto the sofa in Maria's lounge. The sofa had been bought with ill-gotten gains but it was very comfortable. He was asked if he would like coffee or a beer and offered the television remote control When Mike went to the bathroom, he noted that Maria had bought him a toothbrush and put it next to hers. He had a feeling he was going to get lucky tonight.

He began to relax but the vision of the boards with the details of the murder investigations flashed through his mind. He pondered upon the details for a minute but when Maria returned carrying a beer and then curled up next to him, the thought was banished from his head. He found a sci-fi film and sat back in the anticipation of seeing lots of things being blown up.

Chapter 47

Shortly after the murder of Martin Cole, Eve had been at work in the department store when she heard someone call her name. "Eve, is that you?"

She turned to see a tall grey haired man approaching her. As he got closer, she saw that it was an old friend from many years before called Stuart. She smiled and went towards him and they had a quick hug.

Stuart had been a friend of her husband Frank. Stuart and his wife Tina and her and Frank had socialised a fair bit when they were younger. When Tina had children, it was more difficult to get together and then she and Stuart had moved away and they lost touch. Eve had not seen them for twenty years.

"How are you? Is Tina with you?"

The look on Stuart's face told her that she had said the wrong thing. "She died four years ago. It was cancer."

Eve offered her apologies and asked after his children who were adults now. He said that he had seen the articles in the paper about Martin Cole at the time of his trial but when he tried to contact her, she had moved home and he didn't know how to trace her. Maybe they could catch up properly at some time. Phone numbers were exchanged and Eve went back to work hopeful that Stuart would call.

Since the dismantling of their operation, Eve had felt at a bit of a loss. She didn't miss the actual killing but she did miss the excitement of the planning and subterfuge they had to employ. Now she went to work and went home and Sunday lunch with the girls was all she had to look forward to. She was still relatively young and, now that Martin Cole had been removed, she hoped that she could start a new life. A new life with a new man would be good.

The next day, Stuart phoned and they arranged to meet at a restaurant in town on Friday night. That evening, Eve looked through her wardrobe and tried on several outfits deciding what to wear for the meal. She was getting a little ahead of herself. Stuart had said that he wanted to catch up and she was acting like she was going on a date. The low cut red dress was put back in the wardrobe and she selected black trousers and a soft pink blouse instead.

When they had been close friends long ago, Eve had been very fond of Stuart. He was light hearted and funny and would gently chide her for her strong willed dedication to work.

"Relax, Eve," he would say. "Take a moment to enjoy the good times."

They were good times back then. The four of them laughed a lot and Eve could unwind in their company. When they moved away, it was sad but life goes on and she had not thought of Stuart and Tina in a long time.

When Friday arrived, they met at the restaurant at the appointed time. After ten minutes of somewhat awkward small talk, they both relaxed. Stuart told the story of his wife's slow and painful death and Eve gave details of Martin Cole's con which had led to Frank's heart attack. They reflected on their losses but then looked back to the times they had all spent together and good memories returned. It was an emotional evening but it was cathartic. Stuart said he would like to meet up again and Eve said that she would be happy to do so.

When she got home, Eve did something she hadn't done since Martin Cole's death. She took out her photograph album and looked at the pictures of her and Frank, the one at the warehouse and the one with the mayor and, of course, the one of their wedding. This time, the viewing didn't fuel her rage. She could look at them now and remember Frank without thinking about the tragic circumstances that led to his end.

At Sunday lunch, she told her friends about bumping into Stuart and how they had been to dinner and planned to go out again.

"I know we've only been out once but I think we might get on pretty well."

Penny and Dorothea were delighted for her and demanded every detail of their date and their previous friendship. The tea cups were put away and the wine glasses replaced them. This story needed time and alcohol.

Over the next three months, Eve and Stuart conducted a slow and steady courtship. They had each loved the partners taken from them and they wanted to be cautious about making a new commitment. They enjoyed each other's company and found they were compatible in many ways. They shared their feelings and revealed aspects of their lives to each other that they had not discussed with anyone before. There were some things, however, that needed to stay secret.

Once Eve had been introduced to Stuart's children and their partners, she knew that this relationship had a good chance of success. What would Stuart say if he found out about her stint as a serial killer? She didn't worry too much about the question after it occurred to her. The ladies' crimes had not been uncovered by the police and she wasn't going to tell him.

Eve's psyche had not been damaged by the killing spree. It was something that she had been happy to do at the time. Her anger had been purged by the death of Martin Cole. A perfect end to the campaign. Had she met Stuart before the murders, she would not have been interested in his overtures. She would have been completely absorbed by her hate and need for vengeance.

Eve knew that Dorothea and Penny were worried that she was going to suffer some sort of post traumatic stress disorder but she hadn't. For a couple of weeks after they burned their kit, she would wake in the morning and wait for the repercussions to kick in. The backlash never happened and now that she was seeing Stuart, she no longer even thought about the murders. She could see no future where she would return to her life of crime.

There had been some nerves when Eve had met Stuart's children. The stakes were raised when Stuart was introduced to her special friends. He had heard so much about Dorothea and Penny and how they had helped each other through the tough times following the loss of their money and their husbands. The ladies questioned him, quite gently but thoroughly, and, when he saw them exchange a look and nod, he knew that he had been approved.

He could see why Eve had such love for her friends. They had been cautious about him at first but as soon as they were happy, he felt completely accepted into their lives. Stuart thought that, over time, Dorothea and Penny would become special friends to him and his family too. When they left that day, there was much hugging and kissing and the odd tear.

Chapter 48

Dorothea had been slightly blue after the killings had finished. Having a somewhat unusual hobby had been good. Finding solutions to the many problems they faced had given her brain a challenge which she enjoyed. Seeing their plans come to fruition and their targets neutralized was the icing on the cake. She chuckled to herself occasionally when she thought about how they got away with it.

Before the killings, Dorothea had spent her time caring for Eve and Penny. Their enterprise made them all stronger and they didn't need her as much as they used to. That was a good thing for them and for her too. Now she needed to get on with her own life. She would not be going back to the church, her faith had gone, but she did want to use her brain to help a good cause, a legal one this time.

There were lots of websites which gave details of opportunities for volunteering. Dorothea had been in contact with a group who were involved in adult education. As a former teacher, she felt this was tailor made for her skills. She would take the appropriate courses and then help young adults who struggled with literacy and numeracy. The people she would be teaching were often young offenders. Unable to get jobs, these people turned to lives of crime so learning to read and write better gave them a chance to find employment and break the cycle. There was a nice irony in her helping others avoid committing crimes.

The other thing she wanted to do now was visit America. Dorothea had been reluctant to leave the ladies when they had been troubled but things were better and she could take the plunge. Robert and Melanie had been pestering her for a long time and, when she had said that she would travel to see them, they were ecstatic. Rick and Tamara appeared on her computer screen jumping up and down with excitement. There were so many places that they wanted to show her.

As if that wasn't exciting enough, she had received a call from Malcolm who wanted to visit her with his latest girlfriend. Malcolm seemed to have many girlfriends but they never lasted long. She had just learned the name of the latest and then he was with a new one. The fact that he was bringing the present one to her home meant that it had to be quite serious.

"Is this the first girlfriend he has brought home?" enquired Eve.

"The first one since he was about fifteen." Dorothea had met for a coffee with the ladies and was telling them about the lunch she had been planning for the following Sunday. The ritual of the Sunday lunches was not being so religiously observed. Eve sometimes had arrangements with Stuart and Penny was always welcome at one of her daughters' homes.

The discussions took a trip into wild conjecture. Dorothea was already imagining Malcolm's wedding and wondering where he would choose to live with her two or three grandchildren. She hoped it would be close so she could see a lot of them. She would be quite happy to babysit or help out in any way she could.

Malcolm introduced his mother to Alexis when they arrived for lunch. She had bought Dorothea flowers and a bottle of wine. It was the perfect start to what was to be a lovely day. Her son and his girlfriend smiled at each other and laughed often. She felt a pang of nostalgia for her early days with Royston but it was a happy memory. Alexis ate all her dinner, always a good sign for Dorothea, and was genuinely interested in what she had to say. The plans to teach adults to read and write were met with encouragement from both of them.

As they journeyed home, Malcolm and Alexis talked about the lunch they had shared with his mother. "I don't know what I expected, maybe someone who was sad and wounded by what happened, but she is wonderful. To have gone through such loss and be able to smile and laugh and enjoy life is great."

Malcolm grinned at his girlfriend. She liked his mother and that would make life so much easier in the future.

What a strange path her life had taken after the death of her beloved husband. She had met, through the most tragic circumstances, two women who would be her friends for life. They were brought together by their need for solace and bonded further when they undertook the job of serving vengeance on the fraudsters. The killing of Martin Cole had set them free from the past. The bad memories and heartache were behind them. They had jettisoned what was no longer needed but would always keep their relationship intact.

Three months after their final operation, Dorothea was sat next to a youth at the library helping him to read. He struggled at first but she patiently persisted and, at the end of their allotted time, he smiled and thanked her. She was going to love her new calling. Her plane tickets had been bought and, in a couple of months, she would be travelling to America. Malcolm had told her on the phone that he and Alexis were looking for a property halfway between the city and her home. They were going to live together but hadn't mentioned marriage. She was happy with their decision though because it was one step closer to where she wanted them to be.

The one regret that Dorothea had about their crusade was that she never had the guts to witness one of Eve's killings. It was probably much more mundane than she imagined. She pictured Eve striking with furious speed and the victim looking aghast into the face of the tiny woman who had delivered the blow. She preferred to think of her in normal clothes. The image of her in the green romper suit with the goggles and the mask rather ruined the effect.

She missed out on being present at any of the four killings but she was proud of the part she had played. The news that Martin Cole was dead had made her very happy. The end of the operation at that point had been logical. They had achieved their goals and not been caught. Teaching adults to read was a much more benign occupation.

Chapter 49

Penny would often smile to herself when she thought about the death of John Hall, that huge beast of a man taken down by two leprechauns. Okay, he had been handicapped by his broken ankle but it was still a massive achievement.

Laura questioned her once when she saw her smiling to herself. "What's amusing you mum?"

"Oh, I was just thinking about some fun I had with the girls."

In the aftermath of the Martin Cole con, Penny struggled more than Eve and Dorothea. Their husbands died tragically but her husband had chosen death. They mourned the loss of their partners but she felt anger about Derek's decision. She was angry with Derek. On the many occasions when she had thought about following him to oblivion, it had been her friends who helped her through.

The murders had shown her how strong she really was. Penny was still alive, a minor miracle in itself, and now she could face the future knowing she could cope with whatever life threw at her. She could think about Derek and acknowledge his weaknesses but also remember that he had loved her and given her two beautiful daughters.

After the bonfire, Penny was ready to deal with the lock up garage. She returned a couple of times to burn more of the rubbish Derek had accumulated. She took the deed, which was still in Derek's name, to the solicitor with a copy of the will and some identification and arranged for the name to be changed.

Within days of the transfer going through, a letter arrived from a Clive West who was interested in buying the garage. He asked that she phone him to discuss a possible sale and to let him know the price. This man was very keen to get hold of the property and she wondered why that was. Penny would do some research into the value of lock ups before she contacted Mr West.

The Land Registry proved to be a wonderful source of information. Penny had never seen anyone else when she visited her garage, which was one of four sited on a piece of scruffy land. She looked into the others to find out if they had been sold recently and how much they had gone for. The research proved very fruitful. The other three garages were owned by a company called West Developments Ltd.

So, Mr West owned three of the garages, but he needed the fourth to be able to carry out his development. She would not be looking for the market value of the property. She now knew that the buyer was desperate and she would get as much as she possibly could. Penny phoned Mr West and arranged to meet him. In the call, she had adopted her dithery grandma persona but he was in for a nasty shock when negotiations started.

When Penny entered the coffee shop to meet him, she saw a rotund man of about forty years of age. He had a thick mop of dark brown hair and was talking loudly into a mobile phone. He had described himself so that she would know who to look for when they met. He seemed to be a man who was puffed up with his own importance. She couldn't wait to watch him deflate.

"Mr West? I'm Penny Grant; we spoke on the phone."

He stood and shook her hand, asked if she wanted a drink, and then bellowed the order across the cafe. Mr West told her that he had been looking for a garage and that he was keen to get hers as they were difficult to get hold of. The market price was £10,000 but he would give her £12,000 to wrap the deal up quickly.

Penny smiled sweetly at Clive, as she had been told to call him, and said that she had a couple of questions. “Are you anything to do with the company West Developments Ltd.?”

The look on his face was priceless as he struggled to form a word. She carried on, “I have done some research and it would appear that my garage is the only one you don’t own. I imagine that the site of the garages would be an ideal place to build flats or something like that.” She quickly picked up her cup of coffee because he looked as if he might snatch it back.

Clive West looked at this ordinary woman and couldn’t believe what he was hearing. She may look like a pushover but her soft manner disguised someone who was determined to get as much money out of him as she could. As a businessman, he quite admired her. He got over his initial shock and decided to come clean.

"It seems, Penny, you have come to our meeting well prepared. You know I need that garage and you are going to charge me a premium. Fair enough, let's start haggling."

Over the next hour, although the discussion was tough, both of them enjoyed the contest. Towards the end, Penny told Clive the story of the garage. How it had belonged to her late husband who committed suicide after they lost their money to a conman.

"His name was Martin Cole; you've probably read about him."

Oh God, thought Clive, she has played the sympathy card and played it well. He had read about the fraudster and he did feel terribly sorry for her. “£50,000 is my final offer.”

“That sounds very good. Do we shake hands now?” Penny was feeling quite sorry for him.

“You know the lock up garage? Well I’ve sold it. I got £50,000 for it.” Dorothea and Eve stared at Penny open mouthed. She grinned at them and told the story of her meeting with Clive West. She admitted that prior to the killings she would never have been able to sit across a table from someone and negotiate such a deal. “Doing what we did has changed my life for the better.”

The money made her life so much easier. She would keep her job at the accountants’. She hadn’t finished making him pay yet and she quite liked working in the office. Now she didn’t have to rely on her girls and she could give herself the occasional treat. The garage had been the last link to the Vigilante Killer too, so she was glad that very soon it would be demolished.

She looked at Eve who was falling in love with a new man and Dorothea who was embarking on new projects and planning her trip to America, how far they had all come since the death of Martin Cole three months before. They didn't meet every Sunday anymore because they had proper lives now. Sometimes she would go to one of the girls on a Sunday and sometimes she would stay home alone. She was not sad with the new arrangements.

At weekends and in the evenings, Penny was often sat at her sewing machine. Making the coveralls had reignited her love of sewing and she now did a bit of work making curtains for an interior designer. The fabrics she worked with were modern and colourful. She hoped she would never see a green material with leaves all over it.

Chapter 50

Mike and Adam got a call on a Monday morning informing them that they had found a body. The name Vigilante Killer was uttered and they set off immediately for the scene of the crime. The corpse was in some bushes outside a block of shoddy bedsits. It was no surprise when the officer who arrived first confirmed that the victim had died as a result of a single stab wound to the neck. The identity of the victim, however, did surprise them.

"Oh my God, it's Gavin." Mike and Adam looked at each other and then back at the body.

Scene of crime officers were buzzing around in their white overalls collecting samples and taking photographs.

"Do you think the murderer has slipped up this time?" Mike asked a passing white clad officer.

"There's nothing obvious but who knows. This rain that's been falling all night doesn't help. We'll do what we can and pray that this time we get a break."

Adam was looking at the corpse with somewhat mixed feelings. This man had conned women and he had given Mike and Maria no end of trouble. He knew about Gavin's obsession with Maria and all the phone calls and letters she had received. Mike had been scrupulous in reporting the incidents as they occurred. What a stroke of luck it had been that the Vigilante Killer had chosen to dispose of this particular conman.

Following Gavin's arrest, the fraud squad had looked more deeply into his past. They found payments going into his bank account over the years from a number of women. The women had been contacted and some of them had agreed to press charges as well. They now had eight women prepared to go to court but there were probably many more that didn't want to take it any further or that they didn't know about.

All their hard work had been in vain. The fraud squad would not have their day in court but Gavin would not swindle another woman. One of the detectives arranged for the records to be archived and pondered on the death of another con artist. If the Vigilante Killer carried on like this, there would be no one left for them to investigate.

Back at the station, Mike and Adam went to see the Chief Inspector. This latest murder seemed to be by the Vigilante Killer but because of their involvement with Gavin prior to his death, they were technically suspects too. They were advised to carry on with the investigation on the assumption that it was done by the serial killer. If anything came to light which led them to think otherwise, they would review the situation.

The picture was stuck on the board next to that of Martin Cole. Adam picked up an orange marker and started to make notes.

"I'm even less inclined to find the killer now," said Mike. "He has done Maria and me a big favour." Adam looked at him and frowned. "I know, I know, we have to catch him and I will make every effort to do so but you know what I mean." Adam did know what he meant.

They made a list of people who had been conned by Gavin Vincent and interviews began. Although she had not been conned as such, Maria was on the list and interviewed by another detective. She was shocked to hear about Gavin's murder but also relieved. The phone calls and letters had diminished but she still felt nervous every time she left the house.

Gavin's behaviour since they had split up had been increasingly worrying and she was glad that it would all now stop. This man had cared for her and loved her in his way, but it had been an odd affair. She had never known someone who died a violent death and she found herself thinking about Gavin and wondering how this intelligent handsome man's life had gone so wrong.

That evening, Maria and Mike talked about the murder and she shed a few tears. She cried partly at the shock of the killing, partly in relief that the stalking would now stop, and partly for the man Gavin could have been had he not lost his way. Mike was very understanding as she explained her feelings. He admitted he was pleased Gavin had gone because he didn't know how he would have dealt with him if things had turned nasty.

All of the incidents of harassment had been logged by the police. Mike insisted that everything was done by the book. Even though he was in the police force, it did not mean that he could take the matter into his own hands. Procedures had to be followed and reports filed. Mike was glad now that he had acted professionally because it meant that he was not a serious suspect in the case.

A fellow officer took statements from Adam and Mike about their movements on the day of the murder. It was a form filling exercise to appease the top brass but it had to be done. They waited anxiously for the forensics report but, once again, there was no DNA or finger prints. The medical examiner thought that a different knife had been used but he wasn't sure.

The ritual of standing in front of the board at the end of the day seeking some divine intervention resumed. The five faces of the murdered conmen looked back at them waiting for justice. The paperwork relating to the cases was piled all around the desks. It seemed, despite all their hard work and diligence, this Vigilante Killer was going to remain at large.

There had been another review of the evidence undertaken by a different force and then a review of that review. The newspapers used words such as "inept" and "incompetent" when they reported that there was still a serial killer on the loose. The Chief Inspector had been obliged to speak at a press conference and outline the investigation and reveal the lack of forensic clues. It was likely that the Home Secretary would speak to their Police Commissioner to establish that a thorough job had been done.

Mike went home to Maria after work now. He had not given up his rented flat yet so it was not official but to all intents and purposes, they were back together. Phoebe was a happy child and was regularly asking if she could have a baby sister or brother. That might just be a possibility now.

The failure to catch the Vigilante Killer would be an albatross around his neck but Mike could live with that. He and Adam and all the other officers involved had done their work to the best of their abilities. He wondered if in ten or twenty years time, developments in forensics would give them another chance to apprehend the killer.

Chapter 51

Gavin had taken to writing letters and notes to Maria. So far, no reply but she had not sent them back to him either which he took as a sign of encouragement. He liked writing the letters. He could pour out his feelings uninterrupted although he sometimes found it difficult to express what he wanted to say. When in doubt, he said she was beautiful and he loved her.

Gavin had rented a bedsit near to where Maria lived. If he couldn't be in the same house as her, he wanted to be close. When they met, he promised to look after her and he still felt bound to this obligation. It seemed that Maria's ex-husband was spending a lot of time at her house but he had failed in his duty to care for her once before and couldn't be trusted now.

He had not been able to call at the house to see Maria because her ex sent the police to move him on. Gavin sometimes walked down her street and ambled slowly past her property but he couldn't risk approaching and ringing the doorbell. He was becoming convinced that all his troubles would be over if he could get Mike out of the picture. Without her ex-husband, Maria would need him again.

The bedsit was small and clean but still depressing. Gavin had been low on funds when he rented it because he had spent most of his emergency savings trying to keep Maria happy. He had found a job working behind a bar in a local pub. He worked the evening shift mostly which left him free to roam around the streets near Maria's house during the day and keep an eye on her.

The Detective Inspector was a constant thorn in Gavin's side. He was not thinking about the time he might spend in prison when his case came to court, he was not thinking about anything at all except how to get rid of Mike. He had put his thoughts in a letter to Maria saying that if he did not hear from her, he would make arrangements to get rid of Mike. She had not replied so she obviously wanted him to carry on with his plan.

Gavin knew that he had to dispose of Mike but he had not been capable of making a coherent plan. Was his desperate need to get back with Maria because he loved her or because he couldn't believe that she didn't love him? Whatever the reason, Gavin wanted Mike out of the way but didn't know how he was going to accomplish it. He was desperate enough now to kill.

He helped himself to a few drinks when he was working. It was a slow night and Gavin spent a lot of time thinking about his predicament. A couple of women came into the bar and showed a lot of interest in him but he hardly noticed. The alcohol Gavin had consumed would help dull the pain of his aching heart. He walked up the path of the building where his bedsit was situated. The security light hadn't come on. He would have to find his keys and find the keyhole in the dark. Someone was behind him and he began to turn to see who it was.

The knife sank into Gavin's neck and he staggered backwards and then fell to the ground. That was convenient as he was nearer to the bushes now so it was not so far to drag the body. It was not absolutely necessary to conceal him but the longer it took to discover the body, the more the elements had time to do their work. It was starting to drizzle and, if it rained more, that would be a good thing. The killer checked the area to ensure they left no trace behind and then left the area using a route that avoided CCTV cameras.

Chapter 52

Dorothea could not believe what she was seeing on the television. As she stared at the screen, the phone began to ring and Penny's first words were, "Are you watching this?"

Eve was at work and unlikely to have heard the news. Dorothea left her a message saying "The Vigilante Killer has struck again. Come around after work."

The crime reporter gave the details that he had so far. The victim was named as Gavin Vincent. He had recently been arrested and charged with fraud. His crimes were similar to those of Simon Butler, another Vigilante Killer victim, in that he had persuaded women to give him money with promises that he would pay it back.

The photographs of the four previous victims, Simon Butler, Eddie Stringer, John Hall and Martin Cole, came up on screen and they were joined by a picture of Gavin Vincent. The reporter gave a brief description of the crimes the other men had committed and referred to the ongoing police investigation which had, so far, not produced a credible suspect.

Eve checked her phone during her coffee break and was stunned by Dorothea's message. Over the next half an hour, she feigned the onset of a migraine. She would try to carry on working she told her supervisor but when she had to take a seat due to her dizziness they sent her home. When she arrived at her friend's house, Penny was already there.

They looked at each other as they stood in the kitchen and after a chorus of "It wasn't me"s, they all relaxed. The kettle was boiled and they sipped tea as they waited for the breaking news item to come onto the twenty four hour news again, to see what they could learn. Gavin Vincent had been the type of person who they would have targeted. He was very handsome in his mug shot. It was almost like a publicity photo that an actor would send out. His thick wavy blonde hair was a little untidy but that only added to his charm. There was even a hint of a smile on his lips.

Penny peered at the screen and said what they were all thinking. “I can see why women gave him money.”

“It’s a copycat murder,” said Dorothea.

“Another copycat murder,” Eve corrected her. “There was the loan shark up north as well.”

They discussed the latest development and thought that this murder was likely to confuse the police even further. Although their modus operandi was straightforward and easily copied, the devil was in the detail. They had gone to great lengths to avoid being caught.

As the ladies relaxed and drank their tea, they began to reminisce about their crime spree. Penny spoke fondly of seeing the large John Hall brought down by two women. Eve pointed out that John was hardly large when you compared him to Eddie Stringer. When he hit the floor with blood spurting from his neck, it was like experiencing a minor earthquake. And then there was the getaway on a scooter.

"Were you scared when you did the first one?" Dorothea asked Eve.

"I don't know about scared. I was very focused on the job and anxious to get it done. It was only afterwards that I thought about the risk I had taken. I'll never forget the sight of him sat there in his dressing gown clutching the spoon." The papers had reported that Simon Butler's home had been filthy and Eve confirmed to Penny that it had been true. There were plates and food cartons and dirty socks in the lounge. “It was like doing an obstacle course.”

The green coveralls were credited with being a key component in the killings. The shock and confusion the victims felt when they were confronted by a tiny woman in a green romper suit wielding a knife had helped Eve.

“John Hall, in his drunken state, thought that he was seeing two leprechauns,” laughed Penny.

That brought them to Martin Cole. “Tell the story again,” said Penny.

“One last time,” added Dorothea.

“After you boosted me over the wall, I crept into the dark corner and changed into the coverall, put on the mask and goggles, and then went to the back door. It was locked so I picked it just like I'd practiced. It took a few minutes but, finally, I was in and I crept through the house. I remember thinking how neat and tidy everything was. I checked the downstairs rooms and then made my way upstairs."

Penny and Dorothea were hanging on Eve's every word. She would soon get to the good bit. "I was very careful going up the stairs, you know how they can creak in an old house, but at last I was at the top. I went to the room at the front and could hear him snoring. When I went in, he was on his side; that gave me good access to his neck and I pressed the knife slowly in. As I did it, I said "My name is Eve Carmichael. I am your murderer." Then, when I was sure he was dead, I left the room."

"Do you think he heard that as he died? Do you think he remembered who you were?" Penny asked.

“I like to think he did.” She remembered the gasp that Martin Cole had emitted as he died and told the ladies.

“I think he knew,” said Dorothea. The news was looping back around and they watched as the faces of their victims and the handsome Gavin Vincent were displayed on the screen again.

The newspapers soon discovered that the handsome detective’s ex-wife had been romantically involved with Gavin Vincent. Although Mike and Maria didn’t talk directly to the press, their story was told through the quotes of “friends” and pure invention. The articles told how Maria had been swept off her feet by the good looking Gavin after she had separated from Mike. He had not tried to con her because he was so in love with her. The police took up the case and arrested and charged Gavin who was on bail awaiting his trial.

The red top tabloids made sensational claims about Gavin's subsequent stalking behaviour. They reported that Maria and her daughter Phoebe were prisoners in their own home and lived in terror of what her ex-lover may do. They also made a great deal of how Mike and Maria had become reconciled as he metaphorically rode to her rescue.

There was wild speculation about how the Vigilante Killer had chosen his latest victim. Some people thought that the killer had, in some way, become proprietary about Mike Nash and had killed Gavin because he was causing the policeman problems. Another, even wilder theory, was that Mike had worked out who the killer was and asked him to kill Gavin in return for not revealing his identity.

The pictures of the five victims became a common sight. They were on the cover of magazines and the front pages of the newspapers.

The television news showed the pictures every time the case was mentioned. What a strange group they were. Simon Butler seemed so very average and Eddie Stringer was the epitome of greed. John Hall looked like and was a thug and Martin Cole, with his polished appearance and gaunt features, displayed the characteristics of a psychopath. Gavin with his rakish film star good looks was definitely the odd one out. In the months that followed, the reports continued to focus on the lack of results and, finally, the stories disappeared.

Chapter 53

A year had passed since the killing of Gavin Vincent. Maybe the Vigilante Killer had given up. Maybe he was waiting for a suitable victim. Mike had other cases now and was not going to let the killings dominate his life like it once had. In fact, he didn't let his job take precedence the way it once had.

He was given a second chance with Maria who he had never stopped loving. Their divorce had never been finalised so they just cancelled the paperwork and Mike had moved back in. He now tried to get home at a reasonable time and only joined his colleagues at the pub if they cracked a difficult case.

Maria was different too. She had always had a fiery Latin temperament but she thought first and shouted less often now. Asking Mike to leave and moving Gavin in had been reckless decisions which caused so much trouble. She thanked her lucky stars every day that she and Mike had found their way back to each other.

She shuddered when she thought about Gavin Vincent now. He had been so handsome but the man beneath the veneer was at best amoral and at worst wicked. The stalking that occurred after she got rid of him had been truly frightening. Maria had feared for herself but mostly she had feared for Phoebe. It was quite likely that Gavin would have used her daughter as leverage to win her back.

When she heard that Gavin had become the latest victim of the Vigilante Killer, she was relieved. The burgeoning reconciliation between her and Mike could now proceed without the spectre of a stalker haunting them. Maria wondered whether they would make it without the drama which had bound them together but now they were happier than ever.

Mike and Maria were expecting another child. Maria was five months pregnant. Phoebe, who had pleaded for a younger sibling, had changed her mind somewhat with the reality of sharing with a brother or sister. She saw all the things being accumulated for the new child and was feeling rather jealous. When she finally met the new arrival, things would be different, they hoped.

The Vigilante Killer case was to the front of Mike's mind again. He had decided to write a book about the killings and the investigation. He wouldn't be able to publish it until he retired from the police but he wanted to start it now whilst the facts were fresh in his mind. He would work through each killing in order, show the method they had employed in their search for the culprit, and examine the reasons why they had been unable to make an arrest.

The book would hopefully, in time, earn him some money but writing it was also giving him a chance to review everything now that some time had passed. With all the modern technology at their disposal, they had not been able to find any evidence that led to the murderer. There were samples of DNA which had not been matched to anyone that were being stored. There was always the possibility that a sample would be taken from someone in the future which would match up and solve the mystery.

The study of the first killing of Simon Butler had taken a long time to write. This was where the framework for the subsequent investigations was established. He had initially intended the book to be a dispassionate account of what had happened but Mike found himself writing about the moral ambiguity which had been highlighted in many of the newspaper accounts.

The people who were murdered by the Vigilante Killer were bad. They had cheated and stolen and lied. They had profited from the trusting, the weak, and the elderly. Did they deserve to die? Had the killer done the public a great service by ridding them of these parasites? There were many people who he had interviewed during the course of the inquiry, those that had been conned, who thought that they had got their just desserts.

Mike would also delve into the role of the media in the investigation. He wanted to cover the full range of reporting from the insightful articles to the lurid speculation and complete fabrication. The stories of John Hall's fighting girlfriends and the operation to remove Eddie Stringer's outsize corpse would provide a bit of levity in an otherwise serious book.

The more extreme pieces would also be studied. Photographs of men had been taken from private CCTV cameras and printed in the press with the question, is this the Vigilante Killer? The police had been forced to make statements on several occasions to exonerate people who had been wrongly accused. The listing of convicted fraudsters who might be future targets had been most unhelpful as it caused widespread panic. Some of those listed had never reoffended and were leading productive lives. They were not pleased about their inclusion on the list.

There were times when the police were glad of the newspaper's interest in the case. Appeals for information were regularly given space and photographs of people they wanted to interview were printed. It had been hard to read about the lack of progress by the police and the criticism that they weren't doing enough. This book would hopefully dispel that myth and show the public that great efforts had been made to bring the killer to justice.

If there was going to be a big case that he couldn't solve, this was one that he could live with. The newspapers had clamoured for an arrest but, in reality, they wanted to identify and celebrate this modern day Robin Hood who helped the common folk by taking out their oppressors. He would revisit the case when he could, in the vain hope he had missed something, but he suspected he would never find out who killed the four conmen, Simon, Eddie, John and Martin. Gavin, well, that one was not a mystery to him.

60968336R00272

Made in the USA
Middletown, DE
17 August 2019